HEADLOCK

Joyce Sweeney

HENRY HOLT AND COMPANY

New York

Henry Holt and Company, LLC
Publishers since 1866
175 Fifth Avenue
New York, New York 10010
www.henryholtchildrensbooks.com

Henry Holt® is a registered trademark of Henry Holt and Company, LLC.
Copyright © 2006 by Joyce Sweeney
Distributed in Canada by H. B. Fenn and Company Ltd.

Library of Congress Cataloging-in-Publication Data
Sweeney, Joyce.
Headlock / Joyce Sweeney.—1st ed.
p.   cm.
Summary: High school senior Kyle is determined to become a
professional wrestler but his dream is threatened by a loved one's illness
and the dramatic reappearance of a long-absent relative.
ISBN-13: 978-0-8050-8018-6
ISBN-10: 0-8050-8018-X
[1. Wrestling—Fiction. 2. Grandmothers—Fiction. 3. Mothers and
sons—Fiction.] I. Title.
PZ7.S97427Hea 2006   [Fic]—dc22   2005035639

First Edition—2006 / Designed by Laurent Linn
Printed in the United States of America on acid-free paper. ∞

10   9   8   7   6   5   4   3   2   1

To Catharine—I will never forget you.

—J. S.

HEADLOCK

Chapter 1

There are seven of us—including a girl!—spaced widely apart on the hard bleachers of the Coral Springs City Gymnasium, shivering, because the AC is really cranked, and nursing our private dreams of being a WWE superstar. No one in my real life knows I am doing this.

While we wait for our instructor, I look around the shabby beginner's group, scanning for potential friends or rivals. The girl is out of my league, case closed. Muscles and curves, so she could not only turn me down but flatten me as well. Hair like a waterfall of curly gold. She looks tense, like she's holding her breath.

There's a big, blond farm-boy type with a neck as big as my waist, who I would bet is an amateur wrestler and therefore feels superior to all of us. I hope they won't go into backgrounds, since I'm a gymnast and I don't want the others to think I'm gay or just somehow not tough enough.

A big black guy sitting way at the top of the bleachers is reading a book, so I put him down as having friend potential. There's an older guy, maybe in his thirties, who I figure will be the first to wash out. Down in front, there's a little geek, wearing a Matt-itude T-shirt, trying to talk trivia to everyone. No one has a clue what he's talking about, and he has to keep changing seats, looking for a new victim as old ones brush him off. Right now he's next to this unbelievably sickeningly perfect-looking guy who reclines on his elbows as if the effort of becoming a wrestler is only going to take up a little of his attention.

"Did you see AWA just signed David Rocker?" Little Geek says. "They're in for trouble. I hear he shows up drunk and that's why McMahon fired him."

The sickeningly perfect guy rolls his head to the side to view this minor annoyance. "Blow off, kid," he says, almost gently.

Mercifully, our trainer comes in. He carries a clipboard and a cordless mic like they use on TV.

Little Geek jumps up and does the unworthy bow. "Jeff, Jeff, Jeff, Jeff!" he barks, like an annoying little terrier.

Yuck. I mean we all know our trainer is Jeff Broadhurst, who wrestled for three years in the WCW as Jeff Bravura until a back injury sidelined him. Even he seems to think Little Geek is out of line and gives him a snarky look before hopping through the ropes and stepping into the ring set up on the gym floor.

"Hey, kids," he says. He's not looking in our faces. He's already scanning our bodies to see if we measure up. I'm not sure I do. He still looks good, lean and muscular, with the same brown ponytail from his glory days. But his voice is a shocker. He used to growl his speeches on TV. Now he sounds like Mr. Glass, my biology teacher.

"I'm Jeff Broadhurst. I was a professional wrestler for fifteen years. First in Ohio Valley, then in ECW, then in WCW. I've had a total of twenty broken bones in my career and six torn or strained ligaments, and I have six permanent scars on my body. I'm unusually fortunate that I still have all my original teeth. At home I have a little collection of those plastic bracelets they give you in the hospital. I have sixty-one of them. If any of you would like to leave now, you're free to go."

It gets a laugh, but a very nervous laugh. Jeff walks up and down, clearly very comfortable in the ring, on the mic. "There are two instructors here at Fort Knocks. If you hang in, you'll work with both of us eventually.

3

But I teach all the beginning classes. Want to know why?" He looks up at us.

We don't know why.

"Because I'm gentle and nurturing? Nope. Because I'm good with young people? Nope."

I remember now what great promos he used to do.

"It's because I'm the best one here at spotting washouts. And we like to get the washouts—the fools, the hot dogs, the dreamers, the slackers—out of here as fast as we can, because people who don't belong here are a danger to us all."

He pauses and glares at us like we're walking hazards.

He starts pacing again. "Your first lesson. There are always at least two people in the ring. Two people doing really dangerous things together. That means the most important thing in our business is trust. I will be testing you from this moment on. If you can't learn what you need to learn, you won't get a second chance. Clear?"

We make a collective sound like a small animal sighing in its sleep.

"What?"

"Sir, yes, sir!" calls out Sickeningly Perfect.

It gets a laugh, but Jeff just studies him for a second and then goes on. "Okay, I'm not going to have you doing any moonsaults today. I just want each of you to come down to the ring, take the mic, and talk to me. Tell me your name, your age, your athletic background, and what makes you think you can be a professional wrestler. You can go first."

He holds the mic out to Sickeningly Perfect. The guy smiles like, *Well, of course I'm chosen to go first.* He slowly hoists himself off his elbows and glides down over the bleachers. Ever see anyone look graceful walking down bleachers? This guy does. He has the kind of sinewy muscles that keep you out of the freak category, long black hair like an Indian. He must be six-three, six-four. I'm about five-ten.

He takes the mic from Jeff, mounts the stairs, and then, when he goes to get in the ring, he misjudges the tension of the top rope and it snaps down and almost decapitates him. We all, including Jeff, enjoy a good laugh. While Mr. Cool recovers his dignity, Jeff sits on the front bleacher next to Little Geek and picks up a clipboard. Oh, great. He's going to take notes.

"I'm Daniel Battaglia. Danny." He leans his elbows on the ropes like he's just too cool to stand up straight, and cocks the mic at an angle. I could never pull off a stance like that. "I'm nineteen. In school I played basketball, and I was a sprinter on the track team. I want to be a wrestler because I like to hurt people." He tosses his hair back like a stallion and smirks at Jeff, waiting for applause.

Jeff walks up to the ring and holds his hand out for the mic. I never realized before how symbolic that thing is. Danny looks diminished the minute he gives it away.

"You have a nice look, Danny," Jeff says. "And clearly shyness is not a problem for you."

We all laugh.

"In fact, cockiness like yours could be a great gimmick. Promoters will want to make you a heel because the audience will want to see you get your comeuppance. Get ready for a career of one humiliation after another."

Danny smirks like, *I don't think so.*

"Basketball and track tell me you have quickness, aggression, and good reflexes. That's a great place for a wrestler to start. Your comment about hurting people? Well, I don't know, Danny. If that was your beginner's attempt at kayfabe, it was very cute."

Little Geek, who has somehow sidled up to me, whispers, "Kayfabe means it's not real, it's just for the script."

"I know it!" I hiss at him.

"But if you really mean that, Danny, you could be one of the first people out the door because of what I said earlier. So from now on, I'll be watching you very carefully."

Danny smiles in a way that's more like an animal showing its teeth. "Whatever makes you happy."

Jeff writes a note on his pad. "Be careful getting out of the ring," is his only response.

Next in the spotlight is the blond farm boy, who stands at attention in the ring like a marine. "Troy Gunderson, twenty, lettered in wrestling at Douglas High, two all-city trophies, one state, full scholarship to Emery, ranked AA."

Sir, yes, sir. I wonder if I'm going to feel inferior to everyone.

"What made you drop out of college?" is all Jeff has to say to this awesome resume.

Troy kind of grins. "My grades."

Jeff laughs. "That's honest. Do you want to give up being an amateur? You sure you don't want to go for the Olympics or something? Try another school?"

"No, sir. I think I have what it takes to be a WWE superstar."

Jeff makes a slew of little notes. "Time will tell. Thank you, Troy."

Of course, everyone else in the room gets to go before me. The older guy, Hector Cruz, gets up next. He's got a heavy accent, and it's really hard to understand him. I can't imagine he's going to make it as a wrestler, since talking is half the job. He says something about pride and proving something to his son, but he puts the room to sleep.

But the girl wakes it up again. I laugh to myself as I see every single one of us lean forward as she strides to the ring. She has a confident walk that contrasts with the tense way she looked before. Maybe she turns it on and off depending on whether people are looking.

"My name is Ophelia O'Toole." She leans on the top rope like Danny did, and her hair forms a cape around her. "I'm twenty-one. I play racketball and tennis, and that's about it for my athetic background, except I took some dance classes as a kid. I want to be a wrestler because I want to learn how to kick ass, and then I'm going to look up some of my old boyfriends and even the score."

O-kay. Just as well she'll never be interested in me.

The black guy, Ben, goes next. He's got a football background and wants to be a role model for kids. I was right about him, he comes off nice. Maybe too nice.

Now it's the Little Geek's turn. I'm scared for him. He actually does a "move" to get into the ring, holds the ropes backward and vaults his feet over his head. He lands a little one-footed and rubs his hands like he got a rope burn. "My name is David Steele, and I've been following wrestling since I was three years old."

Jeff looks impatient. "What's your athletic background, David?"

David fidgets with the mic. "I think"—he has to clear

his throat—"I think wrestling is really more of a mental game."

We all laugh. Jeff stands up. "You do? You don't think wrestling is physical?"

"If you would let me tell you my ideas for my character—"

"Bookers have the ideas, David. Wrestlers wrestle. Is David Steele your real name?" He's leafing through his clipboard.

David's head goes down. His body gives a little jerk, like he's trying not to cry. "No, sir. My name is Dorian Studebaker."

Danny and Troy guffaw, but none of the rest of us do.

"Okay, okay!" Jeff says to quiet them. He turns back to Dorian Studebaker with a grim look. "Show me how many push-ups you can do."

"Right now?"

"No, a week from Thursday. Go."

The kid lays down the mic and goes down on his hands and knees like he hardly knows what position to get into. As soon as he straightens his legs, his toothpick arms start to shake. Jeff counts with him. He gets to twelve before the shaky arms give up.

Dorian scrambles to pick up the microphone. He's on his knees. "I can get into shape! I'll do anything I have to!"

Jeff has finally found the paper he wanted. "You listed your age on your application as eighteen. Is that true?"

Please, God, don't let this kid cry. "No, sir, I'm seventeen but please—"

Jeff is already holding out the application to him. "I'm sorry. I couldn't help you if I wanted to. You can't be a minor and go to this school. If you really want this, get yourself into some kind of shape and come see me next year. I'll be here."

Dorian clutches the ropes. "Jeff, please—"

Jeff shakes his head, holds out the paper.

Very, very slowly, Dorian slides out of the ring, onto the floor. He takes his application. Jeff says something very quietly to him and gives him a slap on the shoulder. Dorian nods bravely and heads for the door.

Danny starts to chant the na-na-hey-hey good-bye thing, and Jeff whirls on him. "Hey! Can it or you're right behind him!"

We all sit rigid like scolded kindergartners while the door swings shut on Dorian Studebaker. Jeff fishes the microphone out of the ring. "That kid has a lot of heart. If he wants it badly enough he will be back, and when he comes back he'll be ready. Okay, did we get everybody?"

My usual problem. Invisibility. "Uh, me." I wave my hand awkwardly.

"Oh, sorry. Come on down."

I trudge down the bleachers, not thrilled to be following the Dorian disaster, but at least secure that I can do a lot of push-ups if called upon. I pick up the mic, and it whines with feedback.

Jeff makes a gesture for me to tap the top of it. I tap too loud, and everyone puts their hands over their ears. "Are you dazzled yet?" I ask Jeff.

He laughs. "Go ahead, kid."

"I'm Kyle Bailey. I'm eighteen, and I'm a senior at Coral Springs High. My background is in gymnastics, and I've won a couple of regionals."

"What's your specialty?" Jeff interrupts.

"Ribbon dancing!" Danny calls out.

"Tumbling," I say as the laughter dies down.

"Okay, good! Can you do a standing front flip for me, Kyle?"

I almost say, "right now?" but realize that's what put Dorian on the other side of the door. I put the mic down, take a breath, and do the move, with a perfect two-footed landing, I might add.

"Good for you!" Jeff says, making notes. "Some of the moves you already know will be really useful to you in the ring."

"Does he know what a front chancery is?" yells Troy. "Because I do!"

Jeff laughs. "I understand what skills you're bringing, Troy. Just like Kyle will have acrobatics and Danny has his speed and Ben will bring his football skills, like blocking and tackling. You guys will make an interesting training group."

"Yeah," I say. "You can watch all those other athletes sit on the gymnast's chest!"

They laugh with me, and for the first time it feels like we're a group.

"Nice ring presence, Kyle," says Jeff, still writing. "You're very likeable."

"Thanks," I say, amazed this went so smoothly. Maybe he was just kind to me to make up for Dorian.

After that, we spend an hour doing our first drill, falling on our backs from a standing position. I'm not kidding. Jeff explains that the real performer in the ring is not the guy who's executing the throw, it's the guy who's being thrown. What happens is, the first guy just fakes a move in your direction and you throw yourself. Immediately I see why Jeff was happy about my background. So to be safe, you have to basically learn safe ways to fall. Jeff shows us that if you fall on a flat back, you won't injure your spine. If you do it wrong, he tells us cheerfully, you risk total paralysis.

So we spend an hour falling on our backs. I pick it up the quickest. Hector has a hard time—he keeps wanting to put his elbows down first. But he hangs in there without saying a word and he finally gets it. Jeff tells him he'll have a lot of bruises on his arms tomorrow but he's proud of him. Hector just nods.

"Don't be afraid of getting hurt," Jeff keeps telling us. "That's what gets you hurt. Okay, good job. Wednesday, we'll try some new moves and see if you can still keep up."

We all go to the locker room to shower except Ophelia, who is sent to a remote location to change. I've spent a good part of my life in locker rooms, so this feels comfortable. The only thing different here is a counter on the way in with bottled water, several bottles of Tylenol, and hair scrunchies. The ponytail is still alive and well with the older wrestlers. I notice now that Dorian is gone, I'm the smallest. I'm talking about height, of course. Troy and Danny are already building a friendship based on their superiority to everyone else.

"Jeff is gay, I bet," Danny says as he towels off. "Telling me I have a 'great look' and telling Kyle here he's so *likeable.*"

Ben, who has been extremely quiet, is dressed and on his way out when he says, "I wonder why Jeff didn't tell you you were likeable, Danny. Oh, I know why. 'Cause you're not."

"Huh!" says Danny when he's safely gone. "Maybe he's gay, too!"

"Ben Gay!" says Troy, amazing himself at thinking of something almost clever. He laughs so hard he gets the hiccups.

"See you Wednesday!" I call, eager to be out of there. On the way out, I see Hector helping himself to the Tylenol.

Chapter 2

I get home that evening about as tired, achy, and hungry as I've ever been in my life. So it's a big disappointment when I don't smell dinner cooking. My grandmother is French, and if there's one area of my life where I'm totally spoiled, it's food. I was raised on *coq au vin* and *boeuf en croûte*, terrines of this and soufflés of that. Chantal can take something like an omelet and, as she would put it, make it sing. I got teased in middle school for bringing weird lunches—stuffed pastry pockets or containers of salad—but I didn't care. Let them laugh and then choke on their beanie weenies.

Another weird thing is that Penelope, our dog, is still outside. Chantal usually puts her out for an hour or so in the afternoon, then brings her in for dinner. It's five-thirty now, and Penelope is leaping at the fence, barking her head off.

Inside the house, there's no sign of life, except the answering machine flashing. I put down my gym bag and yell, "Chantal? Is anybody home?"

I know I'm a future wrestling star, but to tell you the truth, I get creeped out pretty fast. I worry about Chantal sometimes, because she's eighty-six now and people prey on older ladies like her. No note on the fridge. I feed the dog to shut her up and play the messages. The first one is from my girlfriend, Allison, whom I'm hoping to break up with soon.

"Kyle! Where are you? You didn't say you were doing anything this afternoon. I thought when you dropped gymnastics we were going to have more time together. I'm seriously questioning our relationship, Kyle. I think you need to know you're on notice [*hostile giggle*] because I can't sit around here waiting for you to call. You can call me back. I'll be up until eleven, but you can even call after that, I'll grab the phone so it won't disturb Mom and Dad. But I expect you to call me. Okay?"

Expect and be damned. I delete her and see who got the small amount of tape she left unused. "Mom? It's Juliana." *Oh, great. It's my mom.* Like Chantal, she likes to be called by her name so we can all be equals and friends. I'll never do that to my children. "What were you thinking with this sweater you sent for my birthday? You know I don't like blue. It depresses me, and I haven't been a size eight since high school, thanks for reminding me. Everybody's great here, I have a show coming up. I'll mail you the brochure. And I think Genaro is going to be really successful with these workshops. I think he's finally found his niche with reflexology. Well, I guess that's it. Do you want me to mail the sweater back, or do you just want to send the receipt to me? Maybe that would be best so I can get something I want. Ciao!"

"Ciao!" I stab the delete button. "I'm fine, Mom. Thanks for asking!"

My mother, I'm happy to report, lives far away in Connecticut. I only lived with her for four years before she felt her experiment with motherhood was holding her back as an artist and she dumped me on Chantal, which was the luckiest day of my life. And when I say experiment, I mean it. My father is an anonymous donor. Mom felt that every woman should experience childbirth, so at forty-three, she picked my dad out of a catalog and presto—fulfilled! For four years anyway. Genaro is the latest in a long line of loser boyfriends, all younger than her, all with dubious entrepreneurial tendencies, which my mom helps fund. Genaro was an astrologer when she met him, then he was some kind of herbalist, then he was writing a novel, and now it's reflexology.

"Penelope, stop it!" She's dragging the dirty stuff out of my gym bag.

I dump my stuff in the washer, trying not to obsess over Chantal. She goes out a lot, loves to shop. Maybe she ran into somebody and got a cup of coffee. Except it's not like her not to call.

I decide I'll make dinner. I look in the beautifully stocked fridge and think I'll make a big salad. It can chill until she comes home. There's tuna, a container of cold asparagus. I figure I can boil eggs and potatoes and make a Niçoise. I'll make someone a great little husband someday.

The phone rings. I grab it. "Chantal?"

"No! It's Allison. Why didn't you call me back?"

"I just walked in. Listen, my grandmother's not here, and I have to make dinner. Would you do me a favor? Don't leave messages about me quitting gymnastics. Chantal doesn't know, and she won't like it."

"You shouldn't lie. Do you lie to me?"

Suddenly the hunger and tiredness are overwhelming.

"I don't know. I'll have to review the tapes."

"I don't like you making jokes when I'm upset."

"I don't like you getting upset when I make jokes." *Crack, crack.* That's the sound of my mask of politeness breaking up and falling away.

"Where were you all afternoon?"

"I'm not going to tell you. Would you prefer a joke or a lie?"

Click.

I don't even have time to decide how I feel about that because Chantal comes through the door, and Penelope and I both rush her.

"Look at this!" She holds up something that looks like a butter churn. "I got this for six dollars. Six! The man wanted ten, but I offered to walk away, and down his price came. Isn't it wonderful?"

She's wonderful, with her sparkly blue eyes and her red lipstick. She's wearing a black sundress printed with lemons.

"It's beautiful," I say. She's suddenly into antiques. Our living room is filling up with spinning wheels, washtubs, and old sewing machines. I don't know where she finds the stuff in Florida. It's like stuff you'd find in Pennsylvania or some weird place like that.

"Why are you home so soon?" she asks me. "Don't you have practice?"

"Earth to Chantal. Do you know what time it is?"

She shrugs. "About three-thirty?"

"It's quarter to six. I was starting dinner."

"Oh, no! Kyle, are you kidding?" She peers at the clock. She doesn't wear a wristwatch, says they look "clunky" on her. "Oh, my goodness, you're right!" She rushes into the kitchen and looks at the two pots boiling, automatically turns the burner off under the eggs. "Kyle, I'm so sorry! I lost track of the time." She smacks her own wrist gently. "Bad, bad, bad!"

I hug her. "No, you're a sweetheart. Let me fix dinner tonight, okay?" Seeing her has put back all my lost energy.

"Okay, but tomorrow I'll bake you something. You'll see!" and she whisks off down the hall to freshen up.

I love her so much I almost hate to grow up and leave home. Where would I be without her? Either in foster care or in Connecticut answering phones for a reflexologist.

When I wake up the next morning, I feel like I'm going to die. My arms and back feel like little demons were slapping them all night, and the muscles in the arches of my feet hurt! When I sit up in bed, my lower back creaks like the hinge of a rusty door. This isn't fair! Mr. Corbin, our gymnastics coach, told us gymnastics worked every muscle group in the body. But now I know pro wrestling has found a few muscles Mr. Corbin didn't know about.

I back up to the mirror and find I'm right—demons were slapping my upper back all night. It's bright red from hitting the canvas. Whenever I watched TV, I thought those wrestling rings were like trampolines, but they're not. They give a little, but obviously they also slap your body silly. So I start the day with an Advil and a very long, hot shower. I resist the urge to practice my backdrop on the bed. Jeff made a point of telling horror stories of people who practiced things at home and are still attached to hospital machines. But I already wish it was tomorrow and I was back at Fort Knocks. Coral Springs High School is pretty drab by comparison.

When I go downstairs, Chantal and the car are gone. No note again. She's really getting ditzy lately. And where the heck is she going at seven A.M.? Oh, well, if I'm going to have a secret life, it's good she's not paying close attention. I feed the dog, make myself some orange juice and cinnamon toast, and head to school.

When I walk into the cafeteria at lunch, I can see my double life is really catching up with me. On one side of the room, I see Allison with her coven of girlfriends, all glaring at me. On the other side, there's a whole table of my former friends from the gymnastics team who hate me for quitting. Jeez, can't a guy reinvent himself without everyone taking it personally? Okay, I was the best floor exercise guy they had, but I'll make it up someday when I have free blocks of tickets to all the WWE events I'm headlining.

I hobble my sore body through the line, choosing a nutritious lunch of mac and cheese, mashed potatoes, milk, and cookies. Jeff is supposed to talk to us about nutrition tomorrow so I know I have to enjoy the carbs while I still can. I sit alone at the far corner of the room, choosing looking like a friendless geek over any kind of confrontation. I take out a book, like the other losers in the room, and pretend I like eating alone. But it does no good. Trouble comes to me.

"How could you!" Allison plops down in a chair next to mine. "You just totally embarrassed me in front of my friends."

I look up. She's not one of those girls who gets cuter when she's mad. "I have an English test to study for." I try to go back to the book.

She pulls it down. "I'm IN your English class, and we don't have a test! Are you trying to break up with me?"

Yes! Yes! "No, no. I just need some time by myself. I have a lot going on. Anyway"—I need to get some offense going—"am I like your trained dog, or something? Do I have to do the right stuff in front of your friends so they'll know I'm well-behaved?"

She senses the chasm and steps back. "I don't want to fight with you, Kyle. Let's get together after school today. I miss you." She transforms her face back to sweet and pretty so fast no one could be fooled.

"I have to work, remember?"

"Oh, right. Okay, tomorrow?"

Tomorrow is wrestling class again. "No, that's not good either."

"Are you seeing somebody, Kyle?"

Weirdly, Ophelia pops into my head. "No! Of course not."

She blatantly steals a cookie off my plate and stands, towering over me like a hawk over a mouse. "Well, suppose you call me when you feel like it, then! If I'm still available, I'll go out with you."

And off she goes, fuming, to her table of harpies, eating *my* ranger cookie. I know I should do the honorable thing and break up with her, but it's good to have a girlfriend, and I hate to go through all the trouble of finding a new one. I guess I'm even more tired than I thought.

Before I can even raise my shield again, I see my next appointment is on its way. It's Ricky Olinsky, who was my best friend on the gymnastics team. He picks up right where Allison left off.

"You too good to sit with us now?"

"I'm not on the team, Rick. I feel weird about it. I know you guys are mad at me."

"Not mad. Curious, Kyle. Gymnastics has been your thing since third grade. It looked like you loved it. What happened?"

"I couldn't say."

"Some of the guys think you're secretly training for the Olympics with a Bulgarian coach."

I laugh. "Okay, you got me. His name is Vlad the Impaler. He's teaching me to hang by my feet from the parallel bars."

He laughs, then puts his hand on my arm. "If there's a problem, Kyle, you know you can tell me."

His friendly gaze embarrasses me. People being nice to me always embarrasses me. "No, man, I'm fine. I swear."

He stands up, then sits down again. "I know there's something. Will you tell me someday?"

Wow. I think that's really nice. He is definitely getting free tickets. "You bet."

"Okay." He slaps my shoulder and goes. I feel pretty good until I look at Allison's table. She's narrating, and they're all laughing and hand-slapping, so I guess she's telling them she told me off. Maybe she did. I can hardly remember the conversation.

Tuesdays, Thursdays, and Saturdays, I deliver pizzas for That's Amore restaurant. I like the job because it's not demanding. You just drive around and you get tips and everyone is happy to see you and at the end of the night, the owner usually gives me some garlic rolls or leftover pasta to take home.

Tonight, though, just pressing on the gas pedal

makes my thigh muscle hurt, and I can't keep my mind on my deliveries. I keep thinking what it would be like if I really was a WWE superstar, flying in jets, riding in limousines, people asking for my autograph. I wouldn't just be Kyle, I'd have some fascinating persona like the Weatherman or the Ninja. I'd come through the curtains and my special music would play and my pyro would shoot in all directions and the crowd would jump to their feet, thrilled it was me coming down the ramp. They'd chant my name all through the matches. They'd stomp the floor to encourage me when I was on the mat. They'd weep for joy when I won the World Title, and I'd be staggering around, holding my golden belt, the referee pulling my arm into the air. . . .

I pick up my last pizza of the night. I know the address well. It's Allison's house. Check and mate. There's no other delivery person so I have to do it, but as I'm shoving her pizza into the warming oven inside my little delivery truck with the giant eel on the roof, I decide this is the last time she will manipulate me. I need to come clean and break up with her right now, and I hope she chokes on the pepperoni.

She answers the door in a black lace top. Oh, God, is she thinking of seducing me? Then Ricky sidles up to the door, looking like Penelope looks when she makes a mistake on the rug. I realize Allison is a way better chess player than me.

"Ali really wanted a pizza." Ricky shrugs. At least he has a conscience, but he can forget about those free tickets now.

"That'll be eighteen-forty," I say in a monotone.

Allison counts out a ten and nine ones. Very slowly. "I'm not going to tip you," she says. "Because you're a little late."

I smile with my mouth only, give her her sixty cents, and trudge back to my eel-mobile. Lenny Delucca, the owner, came up with the lovable eel character that represents his company. A moray eel. Get it? That's amore? There's one on my shirt, too. It's hard to have a girl disrespect you and wear an eel shirt at the same time. For a fleeting moment, I wish Jeff had taught us some really good holds Monday, just so I could scare both of them, but then I realize I'm relieved by the whole thing. Allison will love Ricky. He was a total doormat with his last girlfriend.

I get home at ten-thirty with a Styrofoam box of fettuccine. Chantal has already gone to bed, but she's left the TV on, and there's a new gadget in the living room, some kind of dressmaker's dummy. Well, I guess at eighty-six you're allowed to get a little weird.

I fall asleep on top of the covers. I don't even bother to take off my eel shirt.

Chapter 3

It seems like Wednesday afternoon will never come. When it finally does, I walk into the gym and see the wrestling ring, and I get the feeling I used to get when I went to gymnastics class—like I'm home.

I'm the last one to arrive. When I change and come back out, Troy and Danny are already in the ring, horsing around, trying out moves they've seen on TV. Ben is in the front row of the bleachers, talking quietly to Ophelia, who has her hair pulled up in a waterfall of curls today. I want to sit with them, since I'm scouting Ben as a friend and Ophelia as the object of several months of fantasies, but then I see poor old Hector way up in the bleachers, all by himself. He doesn't have a bunch of cool workout clothes like the rest of us—just beat up old cutoffs and a pair of tennis shoes. Hector's loneliness is like a magnet pulling me up there. He looks like he's about my size. I wonder if he'd resent it if I offered him some of my stuff to wear.

"Hi!" I say.

He extends his hand, very old school. I'm starting to like him. "Hi, Kyle."

He also gets bonus points for remembering my name. People often don't. "Quite a workout yesterday," I say, rubbing my shoulders.

"Oh, yes!" He rolls his eyes. "I could hardly get out of bed this morning."

"Me too," I say. "I—"

"What the hell do you two clowns think you're doing?" It's Jeff, running toward the ring like Troy and Danny are on fire. "Are you crazy? Do you know anything about wrestling? Anything? Even if you didn't know anything I would think common sense would tell you not to practice things you haven't been trained for! What the hell was that? Was that supposed to be a scoop slam? Danny, do you know how close you just came to spinal cord damage?"

Troy is standing with his head down and his shoulders hunched, like an angry bull. Danny, who just got the scoop slam, is lying on the mat like he's afraid to get back up. This is a side of Jeff we haven't seen. His eyes radiate fury. His voice is ringing off the walls.

28

"I can throw both of you out of here right now, you know that? Do you even know what was in the releases you signed? I'm supposed to be responsible for your safety in here, but I won't do it if I think you're going to do dumb backyard stuff like this. God! Maybe we should have a field trip to a nursing home where I've got a thirty-two-year-old friend who landed like you just did! You want to do that, Danny?"

Danny shakes his head no. He looks sorry, but Troy still looks angry. Jeff focuses on him. "You. You think Mommy and Daddy want a million-dollar lawsuit slapped on them after you cripple this guy? You want to live with the idea you destroyed somebody's life? Do you know how to think at all?"

Troy's face reddens, but other than that he seems to have gone deaf.

"God!" Jeff walks to the edge of the ring and slides through the ropes to the apron. "That makes me just want to go home and give up on you losers! It really does."

Danny jumps up then and runs to him, talking fast and quiet, clearly pleading. Troy slides out of the ring and comes to the bleachers, where he sits, trembling with rage.

I turn to Hector, who shrugs and smiles. Ben and Ophelia are whispering and laughing.

Down on the apron, Jeff signals for Danny to go take a seat. Then he turns to all of us. "I'm willing to start over with you guys. ONCE. But I will not work with students who are unprofessional and take stupid risks. Is there anyone here who does not understand that to perfection?"

Apparently not.

"Everybody come down to the ring, and let's get to work."

The next hour turns out to be sheer hell for me. Jeff explains that the falling back maneuver we learned Monday is how you take a clothesline. Now we have to learn timing, so that in the ring, our fall looks like the result of someone hitting us. At first Jeff just taps us and we fall. If we get it wrong he yells "Early!" or "Late!" until we know how to fall at the precise moment the tap comes. I'm fine with that.

But then the clotheslining starts. Jeff shows us how to run at an opponent, elbow cocked. You have to run with the total intention of hitting him so it looks good. It's the responsibility of the receiver to get out of the way and make the move. "Remember," he says (and here is where I go wrong), "if you fall too early, the audience can see the move is fake. If you fall too late, you'll get clotheslined for real and you could get a crushed trachea."

Oh, okay. We pair off. Ophelia gets Hector. Ben gets Danny. I get Troy. All I can think of is *crushed trachea.* "Early!" Jeff yells at me. "Kyle, early! Come on! What's the matter with you?"

It doesn't help that Troy, still angry from his scolding, comes at me like a freight train and I know in his heart of hearts he wants to crush my trachea. It would make his day.

"Okay, Kyle. Watch for a second."

Shamed, I stand on the apron. Danny rushes at Ben. Perfect. Ophelia rushes at Hector. Perfect. Jeff rushes at Troy. Perfect.

"You see?" Jeff asks me.

"I see," I tell him. "I don't know if I can do that."

"Everybody else on the apron. Let me work with Kyle."

I hate this. I'm used to being the best. The last time this happened to me was in kindergarten, when we learned to tie our shoes. Somehow, I just couldn't get the sequence of moves as fast as the other kids. Everyone watched for what seemed like hours as the teacher patiently worked with me, the slow kid. Since then, I've tried really hard to either learn things fast or fake a stomachache.

"I think my stomach hurts," I say to Jeff.

"Let's work through it," he says. He taps my chest. I drop right on cue.

"It's not your sense of timing," he says. "You must be scared. Are you scared of getting hit?"

Hey, let's save time. Just cut them off now and hand them to me.

"I'm telling myself not to be," I say, wondering if my face is as red as it is hot. *Well, here goes the wrestling career.* A wrestler who's scared to get hit—that can't be good.

Jeff doesn't look discouraged, though. He turns to the others. "Did you hear what he said? Kyle just made a real good distinction. He's telling his body not to be scared, but it's not obeying him. Has that ever come up for you in gymnastics, Kyle?"

I try not to look at my classmates. Hector, Ophelia, and Ben are pitying me with their eyes. Troy and Danny are smiling maliciously. "Well," I croak, "sometimes in gymnastics you can mess up by worrying about messing up. You have to just picture the sequence of moves and not think about your performance and then it flows. But if you focus on how you're doing, you blow it every time."

"Just like sex. Right, men?" Jeff asks. Everyone laughs. Including Ophelia.

"Okay, so in gymnastics you've learned the proper self talk, but here we added a new element. You have to tell yourself not to be afraid when a big bull is charging at you." He turns to the group. "Kyle has a healthy fear. That will keep him from making stupid mistakes in the ring. But he also has to control it. In a match, you take a physical risk every second. Once in a while you'll get your bell rung or twist an ankle, and once in a great while you'll have a serious injury. It's going to happen to all of you. There are some opponents you'll face who are stiff workers—they'll try to hurt you. This is a tough, tough game. You have to face and overcome every fear. The business is too competitive for you to indulge yourself. Kyle, I'm going to run at you in slow motion, then faster and faster. I'm your trainer. I definitely won't hurt you, right?"

"Right."

"But I'm going to come faster and faster and look meaner and meaner every time. And if you fall at the right time, you'll be okay. Okay?"

"Okay."

We work till I get it. I'm over my embarrassment by now, and I appreciate him stopping everything to help me this way. Pretty soon he's charging at me like a rhino, and I still wait till the last second. "Wow!" I say. "Thank you!"

"We're not done. Troy, come on in here."

Oh, shit.

"Kyle? You trust me. But you don't trust Troy, do you?"

"No," I say. Everyone laughs, including Troy. He's clearly pleased to have terrified me.

"That's good. If I was in the ring with Troy, I wouldn't trust him either. But Kyle, there are going to be a million guys like Troy, and you'll have to work with them. You're not a big guy, and you have to show the big guys they can't scare you, or you'll never survive. Troy, I want you to run at Kyle with all you've got. Kyle, if you fall early, you're dooming yourself. If you fall right on time, he can't possibly hurt you. Right?"

I nod. Troy charges, gleeful at his assignment to try and scare me. It's like watching a big, blond SUV driving toward me. I wait, I wait, I smell him. I still wait. His sweat hits me. I wait. His arm is at my throat. I fall.

"Yes! Yes! Yes!" Jeff runs and scoops me up and hugs me. "Perfect! You did it!"

"Thanks," I say, almost ready to cry. "You're a great teacher."

I'd be really happy, if I didn't see Troy and Danny whispering and laughing, shooting little glances at me.

After that, we have a brief discussion on sports nutrition. I was right, I've had my last carb for a while. Then we do something really weird. Jeff gives us each a stack of white poster boards and passes out markers.

"Part of wrestling," he explains, "is developing your

character. Fans want to think they know you. It strengthens their feelings about your matches. As you progress and begin to perform in front of audiences, you'll see what kind of reaction you tend to get. There are some guys that an audience will always boo, no matter what character they're in. So a guy has to cultivate himself as a heel, learn to take the heat as a kind of applause. Other guys, no matter what they do, they're always a babyface. The audience will cheer them, no matter what. Some of you could be 'tweeners,' meaning the bookers can use you either way or switch you back and forth. Different companies will do different things with you. Sometimes they'll put you in the wrong character, but you have to be a sport about it. My first promotion made me be a cowboy. I'm from East Orange—I don't have a clue about cowboys—but I did my rip-roaring best with it. So today I want you to get a feel for how you come across to others, because it will clue you in on the characters you might eventually have to play. Your best character will be an exaggerated version of you. This is a really good exercise to do now before you know each other well. You're gonna really need to put your egos down because we all want everybody to see us as the king of the world, but most of us look like something different. Okay, who wants to be the first guinea pig? Come on, who's really secure?"

Only Ben raises his hand.

"Okay, Ben. Sit in the front row. Everyone else sit behind Ben. I want you five to write your one-word strongest impression of Ben. It doesn't have to be true. It's just your idea of him. Go."

I write *quiet*. Ophelia, on my left, writes *intelligent*. Troy writes *dumb*. Danny writes *sneaky*. Hector makes a big question mark.

Then Jeff asks Ben to write his own word. He writes *private*.

"Ben, turn around, and everybody hold up your signs."

Ben looks. His expression betrays nothing, but his gaze lingers on Troy's *dumb* sign.

"Okay, Ben, I want you to collect these cards and keep them. It looks like no one agreed about you, but the words create a picture, like a mosaic. People see you as the strong, silent type, maybe holding some secrets back, maybe not to be trusted. They can't tell if you're controlled or if you just don't have anything to say because you're not bright. If I wanted to boil it down to one word, I'd say *stoic*. You're an enigma."

Ben smiles a little. "Enigma," he repeats with pleasure.

"That could be your handle. This is how a character is born," Jeff tells us. "Who wants to be next?"

I want to, but I'm scared. Hector raises his hand.

I flinch as I see the cards for Hector. *Old, loser, underdog, weak.* I write *courage.*

Hector writes *pit bull.*

"What does Hector know that we don't?" Jeff asks, unfazed. "We see an old, weak man who's likely to lose his match. One of us notices that he seems to have a lot of courage. Maybe he knows something about himself that we haven't yet seen."

Hector smiles at us. "Maybe I do."

I can't stand it any longer. "Okay, me."

I literally tremble at the squeak of the markers. This is like the personality Olympics, and I think every card is going to read 1.0. All my life I've felt like I'm lacking in something, some kind of style or flash. I fully expect the word *boring.*

"Okay, Kyle." Jeff gestures for me to face my accusers.

Troy has written *kiss up.* Danny has written *fake.* Ben has written *good guy.* Hector has written *kind.* Ophelia has written *hot.* Hot?

I show them my sign. It's blank. "I don't know what I'm like," I say. "And you guys aren't helping!"

"I'm sorry to be doing clinics on you today, Kyle," Jeff says. "But these words tell me you have trouble expressing or even knowing yourself. What I see is that you show different faces to different people. Great strategy in life, disaster in show business. Each of these people is writing how they relate to you, not how you are. You need to find the courage to, first of all, know who you are, and, then, show it whether it plays or not. It's different from how Ben and Hector are holding something back, because it can still be sensed. You're too much of a blank canvas. When you know what to write on the card, their answers will be clearer. We'll do this exercise again in a few weeks. In the meantime, Kyle, you need to figure out who you really are."

I know this is important, maybe critical for me. I know I really need to be paying attention to what he's saying. But just at that moment I'm having trouble focusing on it because all I can think of is the voice screaming in my mind: *Ophelia thinks I'm hot!*

I wait outside the women's locker room, a safe distance from the door, so I don't look like a perv. She walks out in a red dress and heels, which almost makes me turn and run, but I'm caught, paralyzed by how her gold hair is bronze from the shower, how she smells like some kind of strawberry product she's put somewhere on that beautiful body.

"Hi!" she says.

I make some kind of sound, but it's not human speech.

She swings her gym bag as she walks. "Can I drop you someplace?"

"I take the bus," I say. I realize clearly why no one wrote *smooth* on my card.

She laughs, crinkles, sparkles. "Wouldn't you rather have a ride, little boy?" She swings in close to me. "I've got a convertible."

"Okay." I hope I'm not overpowering her with all this charm.

"How old are you again?" she asks as we step into the sunshine.

"Eighteen."

"Oh, good!" says the brazen hussy. "But you're still in high school. Right?"

"I'll graduate in June."

She holds the passenger door open for me, which I find incredibly erotic. "I'm twenty-one, you know."

"I remember." Now I'm struggling not to stare at her legs. When a woman in a dress gets into a car, it makes you very aware of her legs.

"I'm on my way to work," she says, apparently thinking I'm staring at the formality of her outfit. "I'm a hostess at the Urban Oyster. At least until Vince McMahon discovers me."

I'm riding in a Mustang with a twenty-one-year-old woman. The sheer joy of it finally loosens my tongue.

"I'm in the restaurant business, too," I say. "I deliver pizzas."

Her laugh is how Florida sounds in the spring, when all the birds sing at the same time. "So you can drive? How come you take the bus to class?"

I hope I'm not blushing. "Can't afford a car right now." I don't feel like explaining why my household income is a Social Security check. Eager to change the subject, I say, "Hey, listen, thanks for saying I'm hot."

She looks over slyly. "It was the first thing that came to my mind. You didn't have to return the favor, though."

When it was her turn, I wrote *hot*, which didn't mean much since the other four guys all wrote the same thing. Jeff reminded her that a wrestling show was basically a forum for male fantasies and she'd have to get used to the idea that women in those shows have to be fantasy women. She hadn't looked particularly alarmed by that.

I figure she's had about a million boyfriends and that I must look like some kind of pathetic little puppy in the rain to her. But who knows? Maybe she has a thing for puppies in the rain.

"Turn down this street. This is where I live."

"You get along with your parents?"

She's clearly just being polite, so I give the short version. "I live with my grandmother."

"Oh." She looks like she has a follow-up question but we're in my driveway now. "Look, you want to go out sometime?"

Holy shit. "Yes."

I really crack her up. "Saturday? I'll pick you up? Eight o'clock?"

"Yes, yes, yes."

She drives away, leaving her laughter and scent in the air.

I wonder if this is a dream. The feeling continues as I walk into the living room and see that Chantal has a new hobby. Dolls. There are four of them, sitting in a row on the couch, looking at me like a jury.

"Hello, ladies," I say as she comes into the room. "Something smells great. What's for dinner?"

"I made my mother's gingerbread recipe!" she says, like it is a surprise to her, too. "She used to make it for me when I was sick, and it was oh so wonderful." She frowns. "Do you think that's all right, Kyle? If we just have gingerbread for dinner and nothing else?"

My stomach lurches. Not because I don't want gingerbread (the hell with the low-carb diet; Jeff isn't standing here smelling the spices). But because Chantal has never hesitated to serve unconventional meals and do unconventional things whenever she feels like it. The scary part is her asking if I think it's okay. "It's a great idea," I say, too loud. "It sounds wonderful."

"Okay, good. Good." She glances at the dolls and trots off to the kitchen.

It's because I'm growing up, I tell myself. She's asking my opinion because I'm an adult now. That's what it is.

Chapter 4

I'm always the last guy to make it to wrestling class because of the stupid bus. It makes me feel like a little kid, rushing in with my bookbag, when the rest of them have driven over here in their cars. I know what Ophelia does now, but how do the rest of them take this class three afternoons a week?

Coming out of the locker room today, I see that Ben, Ophelia, and Hector are all sitting together. Several feet away, Danny sits with Troy. Jeff would be proud of how we've automatically divided ourselves into the baby-faces and the heels. I take my place with the good guys.

"What do you want to do tomorrow?" Ophelia asks, thereby announcing to everyone that we have a date. Hector and Ben both look at me like they've never seen me before.

"Well, let's not go to either the restaurant I work for or the restaurant you work for."

She grins. "For sure. You like sushi?"

"No."

That makes her laugh. Everything makes her laugh. I'm in love.

"Take him to Chuck E. Cheese's," Ben suggests. "Since you're robbing the cradle anyway—"

"Jealous?" I ask.

"You bet I am!"

"Where do you work?" I ask him.

"The library."

At first I laugh, but his face is dead serious. "You're a librarian?" I squeak.

"Yes." He looks delighted at my confusion. "I have a master's in library science. I'm the youth services specialist at the Lauderdale Lakes library."

"And you want to be a wrestler?"

"Why not? I like to entertain kids. Vince McMahon basically does a grown-up version of story hour, the way I see it."

"You are an enigma, Ben!" Ophelia tells him.

"I'm gonna use that name," he says eagerly. "I think that's the coolest name. I might even wear a mask."

"No, man," says Hector. "Call yourself the Librarian. Are you kidding? You come in with a big book and clock your opponent with it!"

We're all laughing together, which seems to annoy the heels. They glare at us. "What do you do, Hector?" Even as I get the words out, I see Ophelia making the chopping motion across her throat. But it's too late.

"I just got out of jail," he says. "I don't have a job yet. My brother's helping me out right now."

"Oh," I say. "I'm sorry."

"Sorry for what? You didn't do anything. Here's the whole sad story. Up till now I've been a total loser. I beat up my wife, I lost the right to see my son, I got drunk in a bar a couple of years ago and just about beat a man to death. I went to jail. It erased the crime, but it also erased my whole life. I can't see my family, I can't get a job. My brother thought I should be a boxer to get out my aggression. I was thinking about it, then I found out my son is a wrestling fan. Maybe I'll never see him. But someday, if I work hard, he's gonna see me."

No one speaks. It's almost like he recited some kind of beautiful poem.

Hector helps us out. "What do you want? Not everybody can be a librarian."

Jeff comes in with another guy. I think I recognize him from the brochure for the school. He's Dylan Pike, the other instructor, the one who teaches the advanced class. He's an active wrestler in the local promotion, Gold Coast Wrestling. Lots of the guys on their roster started at Fort Knocks. If we do well, our first job will probably be with GCW.

Dylan, who wrestles under the name Rat Boy, is ugly, scrawny, and scrappy. He wears jeans and sweatshirts with holes in them and sometimes brings his pet rat, Whisker-Biscuit, to the ring. If he knocks out his opponent, he lets the rat out of the cage and it crawls all over the poor guy.

"Everybody in the front row," Jeff says. "Rat Boy wants to look at the fresh meat."

"This is it?" Rat Boy wrinkles his ratlike nose. "This is the future hope of our sport? These are tomorrow's superstars? Man, the business is in trouble!"

"You want to see what they can do in the ring?" Jeff asks, playing good cop. "Remember, it's just their first week."

"In a minute. Let me see if they have any personality first. What's your name?"

Lucky me, first in the row. "Kyle," I mumble.

"Kyle!" Rat Boy feigns horror. He turns to Jeff. "You let in a guy named Kyle?"

Jeff shrugs, trying not to laugh.

"Ooooh!" Rat Boy wiggles his fingers. "Here comes the dreaded Kyle! The unstoppable Kyle-monster! Okay, Kyle, tell me quickly what you do that makes up for your tiny size and your incredibly wimpy name."

Troy and Danny snort with laughter.

"I'm a gymnast, and I think I'm going to be able to train to do some really interesting moves. I think I can be a high-flyer and knock the crowd out with my dazzling spots. And I'm not intimidated by people talking smack on me, especially if they're my own size and their real name is Dylan!"

Rat Boy throws back his head and laughs. "Yes. The Force is with this one, Jeff. We're gonna have to change his name and maybe spike his hair or something, but if he can move like he cuts promos, I could maybe do something with him."

Troy and Danny have stopped laughing.

"Now this one"—Rat Boy moves on to Ophelia as I sigh with relief—"this one's a girl. Jeff, did you make a note of that?"

Jeff nods. "I spotted it first thing."

"Good work. What's your name, sweetie?"

"Ophelia, dear."

Rat Boy gives her a crooked smile. "Feisty. So tell me, Ophelia Dear, are you a true athlete who will train as hard as these men and not expect special treatment, or do you want to be some eye-candy valet using wrestling as your springboard to *Penthouse?*"

"Get in the ring with me, and I'll show you."

"Damn!" Rat Boy slaps his leg. "Two for two, Jeff.

She doesn't even need a ring name. Maybe we'll pair her with Kyle here and call them Hamlet and Ophelia. He can carry a skull. Just thinking out loud here. Okay, this guy looks like a wrestler." He's moved on to Ben.

Ben holds out his hand. "Enigma."

"God bless you. What's your real name?"

"Ben."

"Football in high school?"

"And college."

"Oooh. College. You work?"

"Yes."

A chuckle. "At what?"

"The library."

"Okay, you got your gimmick right. Your name is Enigma, and you answer in monosyllables. Since you went to college, I presume you know what a monosyllable is."

"Yes."

"Jeff, I'm sorry I doubted you. You got a bunch of winners here." His gaze goes to Hector. "Oops. Spoke too soon."

Hector breathes hard. The rest of us hold our collective breath.

"What's your name, sir? Do you have a son enrolled in this school?"

Hector's eyelids drop to half-mast. "My name is Hector Cruz, *sir*."

"Okay, Hector. Down, boy. Tell me about yourself."

Hector's gaze never wavers. "I did ten years for assault with a deadly weapon."

Jeff and Rat Boy exchange a tiny, tiny glance.

"I could do a lot with your intensity," Rat Boy tells him. "Would you care if I played up the criminal thing? Called you Switchblade or something?"

Hector shrugs.

Rat Boy is having trouble maintaining his breezy character. He looks a little scared. "You have everything under control, Hector? Because in this business you have to have a sense of humor. We all talk a lot of trash, pull pranks. You have to know when to be intense and when to be light. You follow me? Can you do that?"

"I honestly don't know."

"Fair enough. You'll find out in your training." Rat Boy seems eager to move on.

Troy is next, sticking his chest out, waiting to be told what a big pile of muscles he is. "You're too heavy," Rat Boy says. "What do you weigh?"

"Two-seventy." Troy is blushing to the roots of his hair.

"Bullshit! Do we have to drag you over to a scale?

You're between three hundred and three-ten. Two-seventy is what you *should* weigh. Get on it."

"Do you want to know my name?" Troy asks. "Or maybe my athletic background?"

"You're an amateur wrestler. I can see that from your body type. You want to tell me you're an all-American? What did you weigh back then? Two-seventy, right? Get on it."

Rat Boy moves on to Danny. Troy's gaze stays on him like a laser. Danny is leaning back on his elbows, black hair brushing the bleachers behind him, smirking.

"Anything wrong with your back?"

"No."

"Then sit up, please. What's your name?"

"Danny."

"That's good. You look like a Danny. What's special about you?"

The smirk returns. "Just about everything."

Rat Boy laughs. "Are you in character, Danny? Or is that your real personality?"

Jeff sighs. "I think that's the real him."

"Well, we have to have at least one hopelessly cocky one in each class, don't we? Okay, let's see what you guys have. Danny, because you're so good at everything, I'll especially be watching you."

"Good."

We get in the ring and start working on a standing front flip, which is the basis, Jeff tells us, for the arm drag, the snap mare, the hip toss, and many other maneuvers. It reminds me of how Chantal taught me about "mother sauces"—there are really only, like, seven basic sauces, and you can make all the others from those. I can see that wrestling is the same. If you get certain basic moves down, you can improvise on them endlessly. The only difference between this move and what I would do in gymnastics is that we land on our back, not our feet. It's so easy for me to pick up, Jeff puts me to work helping the others.

Then we learn some combos—Irish whip, leapfrog, and clothesline—and practice running back and forth at each other like gladiators while Jeff shouts commands. I notice I'm much less afraid than I was Wednesday. This part is fun, because it feels like we're really in a wrestling match, and it's still no problem for me. I'm used to learning combinations and doing them fast without mistakes. Some of the others have painful collisions, but not me.

Rat Boy watches from the apron. He writes on a clipboard. I try not to notice him because it would break my concentration.

"Go shake hands with our guest trainer before you shower," Jeff tells us.

"Nice to meet all of you," Rat Boy says. He turns to Jeff. "This one and that one. I like both of them. I want to come back in a couple of weeks and look at them again."

My heart does a wild dance. "That one" was Danny. "This one" was me.

"And you!" Rat Boy points at Troy. "That weight is slowing you down. If you were a little quicker, I'd be interested in you."

At first, it's very quiet in the showers. Then, "Guess it's just you and me, Ass-kisser."

I can hardly see Danny through the steam, which is fine with me. "I'm not surprised he noticed you," I say, hoping to model sportsmanship for him. "You've pretty much got it all."

"Yeah, I do everything better than you. Except suck up to the trainers."

"I'm not doing that," I say, keeping my tone neutral.

He comes looming out of the steam, finger in my face. "I've met guys like you before, Kyle. You act like a real nice guy on the surface, but all the time you're playing games and doing politics. You've already moved in on Ophelia, and Jeff thinks you're God, and now you've got Rat Boy fooled, too. Well, let me tell you, little man. I'm not fooled, and I'm not going to let a little weasel like you cut me out of my chance. So you're on notice. You're in my way now, and I'm going to take you down."

Ben is suddenly at my side. "You'd be a lot scarier with your pants on," he says to Danny.

"Perfect. You got this trained bear to be your body-guard, too. Doesn't matter, Kyle. He can't watch you all the time." He grabs a towel, reaching close enough to me to make me flinch, and stalks out.

"Don't worry about it," Ben says. "He's all talk."

"He's a punk," Hector agrees. "That kind always cries like a baby if you stand up to them."

Troy glares at us in support of Danny and leaves.

"I'm really not that great at standing up to people," I say, getting my own towel.

"Well, you have to get good at it," Ben says. "The wrestling business is tough."

"I know."

We file out to the locker area. "You can still get it," Danny is saying to Troy. "You just have to know someone."

"But I don't know anybody," Troy says.

"You know me," Danny says. Then he spots us, and you can see the jolt go through his body. "What are you looking at? We were having a private conversation."

"About what?" I say. We just had a lecture from

Jeff about supplements and drugs and what a pitfall they are for wrestlers. Half the guys get hooked on performance enhancers to keep their weight down and their energy up, and the other half use pain pills because of . . . well . . . the pain. "If he's talking about something to lose weight, you better think twice, Troy."

"See what I told you about him?" Danny says to Troy. "What he's really thinking is, if you lose weight there's more competition for him."

"If he's talking about ephedra, don't do it, Troy," I insist. "It's dangerous. Just cut back on the carbs."

"It's good to know how much you care," Danny sneers.

"I do care!" I yell. "That stuff isn't safe. That's why they took it off the market."

"It's true, Troy," Ben says. "Don't use it."

"There he goes again. Gentle Ben. The trained bear!" Danny shouts.

Ben goes over to Danny. He looks so calm none of us even worry about it, until we realize Ben has picked Danny up by the T-shirt and is holding him high in the air. "I'm not a bear, I'm a man," he says quietly. "And you better watch your step, since you're apparently involved in illegal activities."

"I'm sorry I offended you, Ben," Danny says through his teeth. I make a mental note to look into weight-lifting.

Ben sets him down very gently and tugs his T-shirt into place. "Have a nice day," he says and makes his way out.

If we all make it to the WWE, we won't even need a script!

Chapter 5

My grandmother should get herself a job on the show *Fashion Emergency*. She thinks I need a makeover before my date tonight with Ophelia, and she's not happy with anything she's finding in my closet.

"All these shirts with numbers and dreadful sayings!" she fumes, pitching another one on the growing discard pile. "'Bulletproof! Do not hunt what you cannot kill!' Is this the kind of slogan a young girl wants to see on a boy?"

Since I can't tell her Ophelia wants to be a wrestler and loves all those phrases, I just lower my head.

"Oh, I remember when I was a young girl and I would get ready for a date—paint my nails three coats, soak in a bubble bath—and then young men would show up in their garbage clothes, just like this!"

"We're just going to eat and drive around in her convertible," I say, rescuing some shirts she's tossing very close to the wastebasket. "Don't go sticking me in a three-piece suit!"

"As if you had one! Ahhhh!" She's finally smiling at something. A cream-colored shirt I didn't know I had. "This is it!"

"That?" I don't love woven shirts. I'm a knit kind of guy. You can't move around in that stiff cotton. And what if you sweat? Those kinds of shirts show it off like a billboard.

"This color will make you look beautiful! Put it on and let's see."

Maybe it won't fit. I strip off my T-shirt.

"What's this?" she cries. "Where are you getting those muscles?"

Okay, that's not possible. I've only been wrestling a week. Still, I have been hoisting two-hundred-pound guys over my head. . . .

"I've been lifting weights a little." I turn away to button the shirt, facing the mirror. My grandmother is some kind of genius. I put on this shirt and I go from this vague, medium-colored guy to this beautiful French boy with dark hair, pale, perfect skin, and gorgeous green eyes.

"You're a witch, Grandma."

She smiles. "I have a sense of color, that's all. And your coloring is like mine, so it's very easy. Your best colors are gray, this cream color, and pink."

"Oh, good," I say. "I was going to buy some pink things this weekend."

She shakes her head at me. "Men can wear pink shirts. If you had a pink shirt instead of this one, you would probably get lucky tonight."

I crack up. "What do you know about getting lucky?"

"I'm French!" She stands up very straight. "I know everything about getting lucky. Now let's see what we can do with that hair."

I run out when I hear a horn honk and see every man's dream sitting in the driveway. A red convertible driven by a blond woman in a sundress.

"Kyle!" she says. "You look great. Did you get a tan since yesterday?"

"No." I swing myself through the door of Paradise. "My grandmother is French. She put me in this shirt."

"Wow, let her dress you every day." She backs out one-handed, never checking the rearview. "You're very different from the other men I've dated."

I'm smart enough to know that's a compliment. If she'd liked any of the other losers, she'd still be seeing them. "What do you think of Fort Knocks so far?" I ask.

"I love Jeff. Danny's an asshole, of course. Troy's an idiot. I feel sorry for Hector, and I really like Ben. What do you think?"

The wind is rushing at us. Speedometer is reading seventy, and we're not even out of my development. She only drives with the right hand. The left is for dangling and gesturing. Her nails are an amazing pink. Maybe Grandma is right about everything.

"I totally agree with you. Danny's got it in for me."

"He's used to being the best," she says. "And with you around, he's going to eventually come in second. Rat Boy was clearly impressed with you."

I know this is true. "Danny's got more charisma, though." Charisma is an important factor in wrestling. More important than ability.

She looks at me, taking her eyes totally off the road. She has on the coolest sunglasses. "Get out of here! Here, let's get on the interstate, and I'll show you what this car can really do!"

I grip my seat and enjoy the ride.

We drive up the coast road at sunset, and as twilight falls and the moon comes out, we find one of those "fresh off the boat" places next to a pier. This one is called Down the Hatch. Very casual, oilcloth on the tables, and the walls hung with fishing equipment to excite the tourists. We try not to eavesdrop and giggle at the family behind us, who make a point of telling the waitress they're from Indiana and they want to make sure they're ordering a "mild" fish. What rumors do they hear in the Midwest of our rampant, nasty-tasting fish here in Florida?

Maybe because we look like locals—i.e., wearing normal clothes—we get a table on the water. Ophelia orders a glass of Merlot. I order water without lemon. Chantal has always let me taste the wine she drinks, but I really don't like it. Still, I feel a little funny when the drinks arrive.

"This is what you get for robbing the cradle." I clink my tumbler against her goblet.

"It's refreshing," she says. "My last boyfriend was a drunk."

We seem to be on some kind of inlet. The sawgrass is black in the twilight. The sky is purple. A lone white heron is threading down to the shore, trying to catch one last fish before bed. "Is that somebody you want to talk about?" I ask.

"Definitely not."

"Okay. I have other topics. What's a lovely girl like you doing in wrestling school?"

She laughs. "I told you, so I can beat up my exes."

I laugh. "No, seriously."

She takes kind of a long drink. "Okay, since you're going to be pushy about it. I want to work on my self-esteem."

I laugh. "Yeah, right."

"No, I'm being serious now. I apparently have some kind of masochistic tendencies when it comes to the men I pick. I know this because after the last breakup I actually had a couple of sessions with a counselor. Here's my brief dating history: guy number one, physically abusive. Guy number two, drunk. Guy number three, married."

"Okay, I'm sorry." I hold up my hand. "I didn't mean to make you—"

"Guy number four—or as I like to call him, the Grand Slam—abusive, married, and drunk. I had the courage to dump him, but I was up to two bottles of wine a day trying to get over him. So, as the brochures say, I sought help."

"So you did two strong things. You broke up with him, and you sought help."

Another big drink. "Wish I'd consulted you instead. My counselor told me I hated myself and that's why I wasn't attracted to men who might treat me well."

"And this led to wrestling school how?"

She puts the glass down. "I want to feel strong."

Something about the way she says that makes me

really want to hug her. But I don't. "Sooo . . . asking me out . . . am I supposed to be an experiment in whether you can like a nice guy? Or am I flattering myself?"

I didn't think she could be embarrassed, but I can see now I've done it. "You tell me," she says. "I'm really attracted to you. That either means I'm cured or you're secretly not a nice guy at all."

"Can't help you." I gulp my water. "I'm the one who doesn't know himself, remember?"

She leans toward me. Her hair smells like strawberries. "Okay, let's talk about you. How come you live with your grandmother? Where are your mother and father?"

"My mother's in Connecticut, not raising me."

She waits for more but doesn't get it. "Okay, and your dad?"

This is always hard. "Don't know. My mother picked him out of a catalog."

"Huh?"

"Sperm bank. She said she didn't need a man to have a baby."

"Oh." Her eyes are scanning all over my face, trying to pick up my feelings. I can see Ophelia and I are a lot alike. We stay anonymous under the guise of paying attention to the other person. What the heck will we do together?

"Weird, huh?" I need to get out of this before her concern makes me feel bad.

"It must be weird for *you*. Can you ever find out who he is?"

"Why?"

"Why? Because he's your father."

I reach for the bread and then realize it's a "bad carb" and pull my hand back. Which doesn't seem to be bothering Ophelia as she slathers butter on her second slice.

"But he's not. He's just a . . . contributor. He's not a real man who loved my mother or thought about having a baby. See, the truth is—and I've accepted this—I'm really from nothing. My father's an anonymous donor, and my mother found out she didn't want to have a kid. When other people talk to me and say 'my mom' or 'my dad,' I can see they've had an experience I just didn't get." I know I'm babbling, but I can't stop. "I'm like people who are born blind. I don't even know what any of those feelings are about. But that's who I am. You know?" I've said way too much. I can feel my face getting red. Someone comes to light the candle on our table, further prolonging our incredibly awkward silence. Ophelia signals for a second glass of wine.

"Aren't you angry? Don't you resent your parents?" she asks me.

"No! People always ask me that. Nobody rejected *me*. They just didn't want to have a baby. I don't take it personally. The only thing that makes me angry is times like now because I'm so different I don't think I can make myself understood to someone with a normal family."

"If you meet anybody like that, tell me," she says, trying to get me to smile.

"I'm sorry," I say. "This isn't good first-date stuff. You make me too comfortable."

"I think it's great conversation," she says. "My last boyfriend thought good conversation was asking me about other women in the room, if I thought their boobs were real or not."

I laugh, even though I probably shouldn't. Ophelia's second Merlot comes and she picks it up right away. "I was talking to Jeff," she says. "And he said nobody with a happy childhood ever becomes a wrestler. He said it's the modern equivalent of running away to join the circus."

"I don't want to run away from my grandmother!" I say. "I love my grandmother!"

"Okay! You don't have to shout."

I look out toward the water. For some reason my eyes are full of tears.

For dinner I have a Caesar salad, salmon, and green beans. Ophelia has broccoli-cheese soup, deep-fried grouper, French fries, hush puppies, and key lime pie. Oh, and two more glasses of wine. I wonder how much that old boyfriend drank that she called *him* a drunk.

But it doesn't make her sloppy, just a little louder and more giggly than normal. She refuses coffee, so I suggest a walk on the beach, which she agrees to enthusiastically.

Again, I find myself in some movie, you've seen the one, in the fifties or sixties, a beautiful girl in a floaty dress, carrying her sandals in her hands, walking on the beach with some lucky, lucky guy. They don't talk. A light breeze blows. The stars are dazzling.

I think it's too soon to ask her to marry me, so when we sit down on a jetty and she smiles at me, I just kiss her. Did I say just? I've had girlfriends, but when Ophelia starts kissing back, I realize I've never really been kissed before.

"Am I your first younger man?" I ask when we stop to breathe.

"Yep. Am I your first older woman?"

"Yep."

"Can I ask you a question, Kyle?"

"Yep," I say, "I'm a virgin."

She giggles so hard she almost falls. "That wasn't my question! But, hey, probably good to know."

"What was your question?"

"I was going to ask you if you've ever been in love. Because I never have."

Again, her eyes stare into mine. I notice her hair and the moon are the same color. The strawberry smell mixes with the ocean smell, and I feel like I'm drowning. I kiss her again. We kiss for a long time. I don't touch her with my hands, just my mouth.

On the way back to the car she says, "You never answered my question, Kyle. Have you ever been in love?"

"Yes." I don't think she understands I mean now.

Chapter 6

The first thing I do when I get to the gym is look for Ophelia. She's been late for the last three classes. Since we're such a small group, Jeff always waits till everyone's there. In the past, nobody was too upset when the class started five minutes late because of my bus, but now Ophelia has been coming in after me, and she doesn't have the bus for an excuse. We all know what's going on, but so far nobody has really come out and said anything. Today, though, when I see everybody sitting in the bleachers with their arms folded and I see the look on Jeff's face, I know she's in trouble.

Troy is very fidgety. "Can't you give us something to do?" He gets up and starts stretching, like sitting still too long will cripple him.

"You can get a mat and do squats, if you want."

Jeff looks at his watch. Then he looks at me like it's my fault.

"Can I get up and run laps?" Danny asks. I know he's just trying to be an agitator.

"Yeah, go ahead. Just don't wear yourselves out, guys. We're going to do some major cardio stuff today."

"You hope!" Danny sprints off.

Ben, Hector, and I sit patiently. Jeff looks at his watch again. I start to break a sweat. "It's not what it looks like!" I blurt out, like a fool.

Jeff looks at me. "Yes, it is. I've been a trainer for a long time. I know what everything looks like."

Ophelia comes in, already in her workout clothes, thank God. Her hair is pinned up kind of lopsided. "Sorry, sorry!" She sprints up to us.

"It's the third class you've been late to." Jeff looks at his clipboard. "What's up?"

"I had a really late shift at work last night. I slept through my alarm."

Jeff stands up, still not making eye contact with her. "Then you either need to get a louder alarm or a different job if you want to stay in this class." He goes up to the ring without a backward glance.

Ophelia looks to us for support. "Wow. Must be his time of the month!"

Ben laughs loyally, but I can't meet her eyes. I know

she lets her customers buy her drinks at work, and when she comes home she has a "few" glasses of wine to relax. I know that, as her friend, I should be confronting her, but I just can't. I feel so lucky to have a girlfriend like her, I don't want to blow it this early in the game. Especially since I haven't . . . exactly fulfilled all my boyfriend requirements. But that's a whole other story.

"While we're young!" Jeff barks from the ring, and we all scurry up, except Ophelia, who saunters. She's got a lot of Danny in her, now that I think of it.

Today's class turns out to be a bonanza for me. Finally we're doing high-risk maneuvers, which means climbing the ropes and leaping. This is where I know I'll shine. Not like the last class where we did suplexes, which means picking up and dropping the other person in various ways. Needless to say, it was easier for the big guys to hold me vertical in the air than for me to return the favor.

So I'm psyched today. Flying is a little guy's game. First, we practice standing on the ropes. Everyone can post, which means you stand in the corner on the middle rope and use the post as a brace, facing out toward the invisible audience. Then Jeff has us turn around and face toward the ring, still on the second rope. Again, we all ace that except Hector, who has some kind of balance problem. Finally, we get to climb up and balance on the top rope. No problem for me at all. To my irritation, it's also no problem for Danny. Ben and Troy struggle, but they get the hang of it. Hector loses his balance repeatedly and has to keep stooping to steady himself. And here's the rub—Ophelia, who should be doing this easily, suddenly sits down on the apron.

"Now what?" says Jeff.

She holds her arms out as if to ward him off. "I'm a little dizzy. Didn't have breakfast."

"Didn't have breakfast! It's four o'clock in the afternoon! Do you understand that this is athletic training, O'Toole? Do you remember anything I said about proper rest and nutrition? Are you working on alcohol fumes from last night?"

Okay, now it's out in the open. As if it wasn't already.

"Don't yell at me!" she says, struggling to her feet. "I've got a headache, too."

"Okay, hit the showers," he says. "You're holding the whole class up. Come back when you're in shape to do a class. And not before."

I see her wanting to give it right back to him, and I hold my breath and clench all my muscles, willing her with my mind: *Don't say it, don't say it.*

Finally, she takes a deep breath and goes down the steps and over to the Tylenol table.

We're going out tonight. I know I have to say something to her, help her somehow. She has too much talent to throw it away. In fact, I wonder if I should go with her now, like in a show of support.

"Okay, Kyle," Jeff says, ignoring the sound of Ophelia slamming her things around. "You've got the best balance. You want to be the first to try a high cross-body?"

Ha, ha, Danny. Me. Not you. I'm the best, I'm the best.

I hardly hear the door slam as Ophelia goes out.

Okay, here's the thing about sex. Of course I want to, since I love Ophelia, and she's the hottest girl—woman—I've ever known, and of course she wants to because she's twenty-one, and that's what she's *used* to doing on a date. Where I screwed up was on that first date, blurting out that I was a virgin. We didn't do anything that night—well, not much anyway, and now of course she's respecting me and letting me decide when I'm ready, which is right now, but I don't know how to go back into the subject. I mean, can you picture me saying, "Okay, Miss O'Toole, I'm ready for you to initiate me now"? I know, I know, just do it, right? But it's weird to be the guy and know that she knows everything and, like, what if I make some kind of really stupid-looking mistake? I feel like I'm going to bust a move and she's going to laugh or something and tell me how cute I am. So, for the two weeks we've been going out, I've basically been paralyzed. We make out to the point of frenzy, shake hands, and go to neutral corners. No wonder the poor girl drinks!

Which reminds me that tonight, when I had really resolved to be a man and just go for it, now I have to do some kind of intervention with her, and she'll probably not be highly receptive to my charm after that. But I love her, and I know how much she wants to be a wrestler, so I start off at dinner, before she can even get the wine list open.

"Ophelia, we're technically in training. Why don't you give that a rest?"

She looks up, and I swear some kind of little sparks fly out of her eyes. She slams the wine list on the table. "Okay, did Jeff tell you to talk to me?"

"No, but you're screwing up, honey, and I'm your friend—"

"You're probably jealous of the fact that I can drink and you have to get a Coke everywhere we go, *baby*."

Wow. Early in the match for a low blow, but I knew she was a scrapper going in. "No, *sweetie*," I say. "I'm jealous of you because you can metabolize junk food and I can't. I wouldn't be jealous of someone who can't wake up at three in the afternoon and drag herself to class." Clean break. Now let's see where her strategy goes.

"Let's drop it, Kyle." She picks the wine list back up.

Boo! Boo! Nothing is lower in wrestling than trying to walk away from the match. "Ophelia, you know I'm right. You're drinking too much, and you can't handle it. It's interfering with your training."

"I know!" Her voice is rising. "Okay? I know. But I'm on top of it. I just let it sneak up a little. I can cut back. I'll just have one glass now. Or two at the most."

"No, I think that for the first few months of training you have to be absolutely at the top of your game. And for you that would mean you go cold turkey. Because if it creeped up once, it'll creep up again."

Instead of sparks, I now am getting a hard glare. "Look, Kyle. I don't need advice from some little boy on how to manage my life."

Two low blows in one match! Unheard of. But it won't work. I know I'm a kid. It's not an insult if I don't take it that way. I need to get control of this argument, though, get it on terms where I can win.

"Let's settle this the WWE way," I say.

She blinks.

"With a match. You win, you get to control your own life and screw up. I win, you don't take a single drink for five months. That will get you through the rest of the beginner's class."

She blinks again. "You're shooting on me, Kyle?"

Shooting means going off the script. Doing or saying something that's real, not set up by the bookers. Once in a while, you'll see wrestlers on TV depart from the script and say something they really mean. You can always tell, and it's always a heart-stopping moment. And Jeff has told us it happens in matches, too. Wrestlers might agree beforehand, or one might blindside the other . . . and they actually do the best they can to beat each other, regardless of how the outcome was supposed to be. I've never seen that, but it must be cool.

"Unless you think it's unfair because you're a girl." I can low blow, too.

"Are you talking about doing this at the gym, in the ring?" She's hooked, I can tell.

"No. I don't think Jeff would go for it."

She laughs. "Well, I would *love* to kick your ass, Kyle, but what if we're horsing around and one of us . . . probably you . . . gets hurt? If we tell Jeff we were shoot-wrestling, he'll kick us out. You know that."

"We can make it safe. We'll put a mattress on the floor. Mat wrestling only. No lifts, no throws, no punching, kicking, gouging, or biting. Just locks, holds, and pins. Just good, technical amateur wrestling."

The waiter comes over. "Just water," says Ophelia and waves him off. Which means she's already accepted my challenge.

"How do we determine the winner?"

"Shoulders to the mat for a count of three. Or if someone submits."

"Mmmm." The sparks in her eyes turn to heat. "I've been trying to get you to submit for two weeks, Kyle. It's on!"

I don't think I can lose. And you never saw any two people eat dinner so fast.

If you're thinking this is a sucker-deal for Ophelia because she's a woman, you don't know anything about amateur wrestling. Even though I'm bigger and heavier than her by a little, we're roughly in the same weight class, and size really doesn't matter on the technical side of wrestling. Speed, strategy, understanding the pressure points and centers of gravity—those are your tools. In class for instance, Danny can pin and hold Ben, even though Ben's much bigger. Ophelia and I already know we're fairly evenly matched. We both have elastic joints, so we can slip-slide out of holds. We're both quick and intuitive. If anything, she has the advantage. Since women have that freakishly low center of gravity, they're actually harder to pin down than we are. So it's going to be interesting.

Ophelia drags a mattress to the middle of her living room. Her cat, Taser, runs for the hills, sensing something weird is about to happen.

"Boo!" I say. "You can't wear a bikini. I can't function with a hard-on!"

"You didn't say anything in the rules about ring attire," she says with a wicked smile.

It's a double disadvantage since I'm in jeans and have no mobility. "At least let me wrestle in my underwear, then," I say.

She giggles. "Yeah, but I think that's going to erase my brilliant strategy. Now I'll be . . . um . . . distracted, too."

"Okay, somebody has to ask this," I say, trying not to laugh. "You want to start in top position or bottom position?"

She laughs. "Let's see if you can guess."

I get on the bottom.

Ophelia counts to three, and we go. I muscle out, get her shoulders, and swing her on her back. She knows enough to go with the flow and uses the momentum to roll right back up, meanwhile swinging a lovely leg behind my knees and sweeping me off balance. I land on my seat and she tries to power me down, but I'm locked. Meanwhile, I bear-hug her and bridge up, pulling her over my head. I swing around and straddle her. She kicks out easily. It's a weird vibe. We're sort of laughing and growling at the same time. I do have a massive hard-on by this time, but I can only hope she has a similar problem.

We're facing off again. This time I go for her legs and try to pull her down that way. Big mistake. It's that freakish center of gravity. She's like the Rock of Gibraltar, and by putting my head down, I've made it simple for her to push my face right to the mat. Now she's on top of me, and I'm facedown with zero leverage. Crap. I have to win this, for her own good!

With a mighty roar, I manage to get my arms into position to do the mother of all push-ups, lifting both of us off the mattress. I try to shake her off, but I guess she's ridden wilder mustangs than me. My arms are starting to give, so I flip myself around under her. At least I'm face up, albeit still pinned.

The evil thing starts counting on me. "One, two . . ."

I hike one arm up in the air to break the count. I try for a kick-out, but she's got one of her Amazon legs on top of mine. Then she starts working on my upraised arm, pushing it back to the mat. Damn, she's going to win! I have to think.

She's leaning forward, putting most of her weight on my chest. Her face is close to mine. I frantically think of our rules. I can't cheat, but I have to think of something. "One," she says. "Two—"

"I love you," I whisper.

Every muscle in her body goes slack with the shock. I slide out and roll her up fast. "One, two, three!"

I let her go, and she flies into a rage and is all over me, breaking several of our ground rules.

"Wait a minute!" I say, trying to defend all my most vulnerable body parts at once. "Wait! I didn't just say that just to win the match. I meant it! I meant it!"

She stops whaling on me and sits back on her heels, breathing hard. "Are you sure?"

"Yeah." I check myself for bleeding or other damage. "Okay, I timed it to win the match. But I meant it, Ophelia. If I didn't, why would I be fighting to keep you sober in the first place?"

"Huh," she says. "All right, if that's how it is, I guess I feel the same way about you."

"Okay."

"All right."

"Glad we settled it."

"Yeah." She swipes wet curls off her neck. "So. Any questions?"

"Yeah."

"What?"

"Have you got condoms in this house?"

She giggles. "I thought you'd never ask."

We're doing it again. In class, I mean. The character exercise. It's three weeks in, and I'm supposed to know who I am now. Markers are squeaking behind me. Jeff is standing over me. "Come on, Kyle. You know something about yourself. What have you learned in training?"

I write the one word I know is true. Then I turn to face the jury.

Ben has written *overachiever*. Danny has written *hot dog*. Troy has written *show-off*. Ophelia, my lover, has written *ruthless competitor*. Hector has written *star*.

I shiver. They're still not all flattering, but this time they're all true. And they add up to something. They can see me. I'm visible.

Jeff is grinning because the word I've written agrees with the others. He holds it up for them to see.

Ambitious.

Chapter 7

In six short weeks, I learn how to do three kinds of suplexes, master the one-handed chokeslam (harder than you think when your opponents are almost all heavier than you), and learn how to do punches and kicks that look like they connect without connecting. I've found my best move—the frog splash. It's a leap, naturally, and as you leap, you have to splay out your arms and legs. It creates a beautiful, hanging in the air, soaring like a flying squirrel, kind of effect, and I get such height with mine that it really is breathtaking. Most wrestlers, Jeff says, find a move that they consistently do best, and that becomes their signature, the move they always use to finish a match. For reasons unknown, I'm still working on a shooting star; so far I overrotate and land on my ass. Danny's shooting star is beautiful, which worries me since Rat Boy is coming back to evaluate us tomorrow.

In the same six weeks, Ophelia has also taught me a lot of moves I never knew before, and my grandmother has switched from baby dolls to Barbie dolls. I'm a little worried about her. But right now I'm much more worried about "Bartleby, the Scrivener." I haven't read it, I have no clue what a scrivener is, and even though my hand is not in the air, Mr. Chavez has just called on me.

"Mr. Bailey? Can you explain how Bartleby typifies the concept of the antihero?"

"Huh?" I used to have a solid 4.0 here in AP English. I really did.

Mr. Chavez used to be my friend. But they turn on you quickly when you stop reading their books and kissing their asses. "Which word did you not understand, Mr. Bailey?"

Honesty is really not the best policy, but it comes to me naturally. "I understood the words, sir. I just didn't read the story."

Naturally, the whole class gets energized by this. They all swivel in their chairs, get comfortable for the show. I'd do the same if I were them.

"And why not?"

Being a secret wrestler will not be a good answer, even if it is the truth. "I'm having problems at home."

My loyal friends respond with a chorus of boos and a couple of "yeah, rights." But Mr. Chavez looks like he *might* buy it. "Please stay after class, Mr. Bailey," he says. My fans go wild with "uh-ohs" and "look outs," like I'm gonna get paddled or something. I keep my head down and listen to the rest of the discussion. It sounds like Bartleby is some kind of passive-aggressive type. They never talk about what a scrivener is.

"Okay, Kyle, what's really going on?" Mr. Chavez asks when we're alone.

"Like I said"—I shift my feet like a guilty little kid—"problems at home. My grandmother's been sick."

"What's wrong with her?"

"I think it's just the flu or something, but I have to help out more at home, and I just couldn't get my reading done last night."

Mr. Chavez looks up and clearly tries to read me. He doesn't want to lean on a kid with a sick granny, but he doesn't want some guy yanking him either.

"You live alone with your grandmother?"

"Yes, sir."

"Where are your parents?"

That's a good question. "My father doesn't exist, and my mother is in Connecticut, finding herself."

He frowns to show he doesn't approve of that. "Okay,

Kyle, but please don't let your average slip now, right before graduation. You've been one of my best students all year. Is that why you quit the gymnastics team? To help out your grandmother?"

I glance up to check for lightning bolts that might be coming down. "Sort of."

"Well, that's a shame. You know you have to take care of your own needs, too. What's your grandmother going to do when you go off to college?"

Fill the house with Barbie dolls and probably take a lover half her age.

"She's all right, sir. It's just right now, when she's sick—"

"Okay, Kyle. Just read the story, please. It'll be on the final." Teachers always look like they're going to drop from exhaustion at the end of these little sessions. It makes me wonder why they put out the effort in the first place.

"Yes, sir, I will." I really will. I want to know what a scrivener is.

God doesn't punish us with thunderbolts. He makes our lies come true. The moment I walk in the door, I know something is wrong. For one thing, Penelope hasn't been let out all day, and she practically knocks me down as she bolts out the door. Since she's unleashed, I stand in the doorway and watch her as she squats by our mailbox. While I'm standing there, I hear the TV blaring in the living room. Chantal never used to watch TV. In fact, she always made rude comments when I was watching it. I let Penelope (much calmer now) in and circle the set. It's TV Land or something, some ancient rerun of *The Andy Griffith Show*, the whistling theme song cranked up so high it hurts my ears.

Meanwhile, Penelope is barking her head off, trying to tell me something. I follow her into the kitchen and she shows me her empty food bowl, with an ant crawling in it. Some kind of trapdoor opens in my mind, sucking me into total panic. Something has happened to Chantal! Some intruder came in and murdered her . . . and then locked the front door behind him? "Chantal!" I scream over the TV. There's no answer.

I can feel the panic rising in my chest, similar to when Troy puts me in a rear chinlock. My heart is hammering, but I'm scared to go in the back rooms of the house. I just stand there in the kitchen, calmly washing Penelope's bowl and fixing her food. I'm not ready to see or know anything else yet.

The telephone rings. I grab it, because I don't want to be alone. "Hello?"

"Hello, is Mrs. Chantal Bailey there?"

"I'm not sure. I just got home. Can I take a message?"

"Who is this?"

"This is her grandson."

"Do you live with Mrs. Bailey?"

"Yes, I—" Now I want to get off the phone.

"Are you eighteen years of age?"

"Yes. Look, I'll call you—"

"This is Donna from Florida Power and Light. I need to know whether your grandmother sent in her check in the amount of $375.20 to bring your account up to date. We—"

"What are you talking about?" I yell because my adrenaline is stuck. "My grandmother always pays her bills on time. Early, even. She used to be a bookkeeper!"

"Mr. Bailey, your account is three months past due. We can't continue to provide you with service unless—"

I hang up. I have no space for that crisis in the middle of this crisis. I run down the hall and find Chantal sitting up in bed in her lace-trimmed pajamas, making paper snowflakes, the kind you make in kindergarten by folding the paper and cutting out little snippets. There's a snowdrift of paper scraps on the bedspread.

"Look at this!" She looks up at me and grins. "Who says it never snows in Florida?"

I just stand there, my hand over my heart, trying to urge it to slow down, trying to get my adrenal glands to quit pumping chemicals. Jeff says you can use your mind to control your body chemistry to be strong and effective, not panicky and inconsistent. What a crock of shit! "What are you doing in bed? Do you know you didn't feed the dog? Is our electric bill overdue?"

She scrunches her face. "What? One thing at a time."

I'm so confused. I feel like there's no up or down, nothing to grab on to. "They called from the power company. They said our bill is overdue."

"Oh, yes, that mean woman! If she can't take a nicer tone, I'm not going to pay her a penny!"

"Are all the other bills okay?" Now I have a cold sweat breaking out.

"They always call if there's a problem," she says. "I think some of them make it up just to have something to do."

They always call? I wonder if I should call a doctor or something. Maybe she's having a stroke. "Did you eat anything today?"

She looks into the middle distance. "Today? What is today?"

"I'll be back," I say and stumble out. I need to believe Jeff is right, that I can control my chemistry and be effective. I force myself to breathe deeply and move slowly. I go out to the mailbox. It's stuffed full of about three days' worth of mail. There are a lot of second notices and one final notice. And about a million solic-itations from charities.

When I come back in, Chantal has gotten up and come into the living room, her hair flying in all directions. She looks at the TV. "Gilligan's Island," she says to herself.

"Where's your checkbook, Grandma?"

She frowns. "Do you need money?"

"No, I just want to see it."

She frowns harder. "I don't know where it is right now. . . ."

I feel so helpless I just want to lie down on the floor, but something holds me up. "Maybe in your purse?"

"Oh, yes, probably." She is way more interested in Gilligan's Island than anything I have to say. She looks like a little kid, sitting there in her jammies.

I find the checkbook. There's a balance of over ten thousand dollars. I know her income just covers our expenses, so she obviously hasn't been paying bills. It looks like for the past three months, she's ignored our bills and just given ten- and fifteen-dollar contributions to whichever charities sent her a letter. The mail is full of appreciation gifts—an American flag, a cross from the Holy Land, lots and lots of address labels. I spend an hour paying bills, then cook dinner for both of us and wash the dishes. I make sure Chantal takes her blood pressure medicine. I'm tempted to pop one myself, but I don't do it. Then I settle her into bed, take a shower, and read one page of "Bartleby" before I fall asleep on the couch.

* * *

I realize the next morning that I was supposed to call Ophelia, but there's no time. I have to make sure Chantal gets up, dresses, and eats breakfast, and then I have to feed the dog.

Chantal is irritated with me and all the questions I ask her. "You didn't have to pay all those bills," she says. "I would have done it."

Maybe it was just a weird event and she's normal now. Maybe I can just forget it. "Could you do some laundry for me today? I don't have any clean clothes."

"Sure." She feeds Pop-Tart pieces to the dog.

It was all a dream, I tell myself. I read "Bartleby" on the bus on the way to school and do fairly well, I think, on my English final. I call Ophelia on my lunch break.

"I'm sorry," I say. "I had some problems last night."

"What's her name?"

I just know I've slipped into a parallel universe. Ophelia's never said an unkind word to me. "Her name is Grandma! And she wasn't feeling well."

"Why didn't you call me? I would have come over and helped you."

"I don't know. I wasn't thinking clearly." Even if I was, I would never have asked her. The thought wouldn't even have crossed my mind.

"Well, I guess if you're telling the truth, I forgive you."

"If!"

"And anyway, I want to cheer for you today. I really hope you get the spot in the show and not Danny."

"It could be Troy, too. He's got some power moves that kill, and he's dropped a lot of weight. They both work out every night in the gym while I'm taking care of old ladies and reading 'Bartleby, the Scrivener.'"

"Oh, I love that story!"

I'm surprised she knows it. I mean, I know she's smart, I just didn't think she was an intellectual type. I realize we've concentrated too much on the physical part of our relationship. Another thing for the to-do list. "Why would a grown man call himself Ginger Nut?" I say, hoping to smooth out our little fight with humor.

She laughs her magic laugh. "Maybe that was a cool handle a hundred years ago. Anyway, I don't remember that part. I just remember him preferring not to."

"Yeah. Rebellion is good in any century."

"Okay, I'll see you this afternoon."

"Okay. . . . " I want to say I love you, because I do, but I choke on it.

She doesn't sense my hesitation or she's impatient with it. The line goes dead.

I call Chantal after school. She sounds perfectly fine and asks if I want beef stew for dinner. My adrenal glands are totally at rest now. Maybe I can do well at my tryout after all. I don't know what Rat Boy is going to ask us to do. If he just puts us in the ring and has us do spots, I can win this. If he wants to watch us wrestling mock matches, then everything will depend on who I get paired with. Hector, Ophelia, and Ben would all put me over, throw the whole match toward my best moves, and let me win. Troy and Danny would both try to make me look bad, and they have the size and power to do it.

But when I get to Fort Knocks, late as usual, I find everyone—Ophelia, Jeff, Rat Boy, everyone—crouching on the floor, staring at something that looks like a beached whale. It's Troy. His face is pale gray. Then I hear the sirens coming, and my adrenals are off to the races again.

Chapter 8

Rat Boy and Jeff act like they've seen this kind of thing before. Jeff is taking Troy's pulse, and Rat Boy is digging in Troy's gym bag. Troy is breathing really hard, drops of sweat breaking out on his face.

"A hundred twenty-nine!" Jeff calls to Rat Boy. "Jesus."

Rat Boy has dug out the culprit. Troy's bottle of pills. "Ephedra!" he spits.

"Damn it" is Jeff's response. "Troy, take really deep breaths for me. Don't hold your breath." He talks over his shoulder to us. "Didn't you morons listen to me the first week? When I talked about performance enhancers? You think I make this stuff up?"

The rest of us look at Danny, who pushed the stuff on Troy. All the color has drained out of his face. "Is he having a heart—"

Rat Boy jumps up and claps his hand over Danny's mouth. "You're gonna be fine, Troy. It's just a rapid heartbeat. You calm down, and you can slow it down." To Danny he mutters, "Don't go into health care, kid."

Finally the EMTs are here. "Outta the way!" they yell at us.

Everyone backs up, except Jeff who hangs on to Troy's hand. "Ephedra," he says to the guy pulling a blood pressure cuff apart. "He was doing warm-ups and he collapsed. His pulse is over one-twenty."

The EMT nods. "What's your name, son?"

"Troy?" He sounds like he isn't sure.

"Two hundred over one-fifteen," the EMT shouts to another guy, who is looking at the pill bottle and writing things down. "How many of those pills did you take today, Troy?"

Troy's eyelids flutter. "Six. I wanted . . . we have tryouts."

"Start an IV on him. You're gonna miss your tryouts, Troy. We need to take you to the hospital and get you stabilized."

"Oh, God." Troy closes his eyes.

"We're going to Coral Springs Medical Center," the EMT says to Jeff while a female EMT sticks an IV in Troy's wrist. "Can somebody come along?"

"Yeah, I will." Jeff jumps up and grabs Troy's gym bag.

Like ants, working from a central brain, everyone lifts Troy and puts him on a board, which they load onto a gurney.

"Call me on my cell!" Rat Boy yells after Jeff as they all pile out the door.

We all drift to the doorway and watch them load Troy in the back. Ophelia starts to cry. Jeff jumps up into the passenger seat of the ambulance. I put my arm around Ophelia. Two of the EMTs get in the back with Troy, and the driver slams the door on him and jumps up into his seat. Lights and sirens go crazy. The ambulance has to honk repeatedly to get into traffic, but finally they go onto University Drive and turn north toward the hospital, which is just a couple of blocks away. We all stand there watching and listening until the sound of the siren fades away. I shiver. Jeff told us the first day that if we stay in the wrestling business, we'll get used to ambulance rides and ERs. It didn't seem real when he said it. Now it does.

We all drift back into the gym, where Rat Boy is turning on his cell phone and propping it up near the ring. "Okay, show's over," he says to us. "Who wants to go first?"

We all just stare at him. "Are you out of your mind?" Danny asks him. "That's our friend. He just collapsed. You think we're going to perform for you now?" *Yeah, now you're concerned, after you caused this.*

Ophelia's crying has wound down. She pulls away from me and sprints toward the bathroom.

"I think you will if you want to be in my show," he says. "Any of you guys remember or hear about a wrestler named Johnny Dagger?"

"I've heard of him," I say. "He was in ECW. He died a couple of years ago."

"He wrestled here in my promotion after ECW. He died in the ring, in the middle of a show. He was fond of mixing alcohol with steroids. I should have fired him, but I loved the guy, and he wanted to keep working. He collapsed in the middle of a match with me. All of us—the fans, the wrestlers, the referees—we all watched the ambulance come and take him away. Only it wasn't like Troy here. We knew John wasn't coming back. There were three more matches on the card. What do you think happened?"

"You finished the show like little troupers 'cause you didn't want to refund the ticket money. And you want us to think that was heroic," Danny says.

"We finished the show because it would have dishonored Johnny and our profession if we all gave in to our feelings." Rat Boy has never looked so serious. "If you don't get that you have no business here."

Ben glances at me. He and the rest of them don't seem to get it, but I agree with Rat Boy. I try to get it into words. "Not because wrestling is important," I say. "But because going on is important."

"You are the biggest ass kisser in the world," Danny says to me.

"No, he's not. He just gets it," Rat Boy says. "All a wrestler has is his heart, his will to go on. That's what the fans come for, because it helps them remember their heart and their will to go on. These little dramas we put on are stories about courage. If you can't live it, you shouldn't play the part either."

Ophelia is back from the bathroom. She's washed her face but still looks fragile in a way I've never seen her. I wish she had heard all this. I would have liked to know her opinion.

"But"—Rat Boy's tone lightens up—"it doesn't matter if you get it or not. Today is your tryout day, and it's the only chance you'll get to work a real promotion for a long time. Your buddy Troy is going to live, I promise you. I've seen enough collapses to work in a hospital myself. Meanwhile, this is your shot. If you'd rather go home and light a candle, leave now."

Nobody moves. But no one looks too thrilled either. I have the really sick thought that I have an advantage here because everyone else is more upset than me. So it makes me wonder. Is a great wrestler really the guy with the most heart? Or the guy with no heart at all?

* * *

Rat Boy decides we will wrestle ten-minute matches in pairs. We have a few minutes to lay out our moves, and then we start. Since we're one guy short, Rat Boy goes first with Hector. I figure he chooses Hector to help him out, since he probably knows from Jeff, Hector is the worst wrestler in our group. They confer for a few minutes on the apron—actually Rat Boy talks and Hector nods—then they get in the ring and do a short back-and-forth program. Lots of easy moves, clotheslines and bulldogs. Rat Boy gives Hector a couple of German suplexes, and Hector lands perfectly and "sells" the pain. Then Hector delivers yet another clothesline, and while Rat Boy staggers to his feet, Hector scrambles to the top rope for his high-risk finish. Trouble is, Hector can't straighten his legs on the top rope without losing his balance, so he keeps bending over and resetting himself. Meanwhile Rat Boy is forced to stagger around longer than any human being should have to. At one point he slyly glances at his watch to make us laugh. Finally, Hector is balanced. Rat Boy turns toward him and Hector tries to leap into a high cross body, but he goes too high, and his torso hits Rat Boy across the face and nearly smothers him as they lie on the canvas. Rat Boy taps the mat frantically, yelling "I can't breathe!" into Hector's stomach. Hector rolls off and stands with his head down.

Rat Boy gets up, takes a few deep breaths. "Listen, Hector, I know you feel bad about almost killing me, but really that was not so bad. You gotta work on your balance. Before class starts, come in here and practice balancing on the ropes. Work on the second rope if you have problems with the top one. And your aim was off, but I think that was because you got upset with yourself. Even when you're screwing up you gotta stay calm or you'll mess up worse."

"Yeah." Hector has heard all this before.

"Let me tell you what you did right. You remembered the whole program. Your timing was good, you sold your spots very well. And you took the Germans without getting the wind knocked out of you. The fact that you can *take* punishment makes you more valuable than the guys who just dish it out. You might want to think about specializing in hard core, where you can show off that great pain threshold you have."

Finally, Hector's head is up. "Thanks, man."

Rat Boy seems so much like Jeff it surprises me. I mean we all know Hector isn't going to be chosen for the show, but it was nice how Rat Boy was really coaching him and building him up. I've never seen a sport before where there's so much competition but at the same time where everyone takes care of everyone else.

"Okay, I wanna see Ben versus Ophelia. Map it out, guys. Think about your strengths and weaknesses. Make each other look good."

While Ben and Ophelia huddle, Danny and I exchange a wary glance. We're going to be partners, and neither one of us is happy about that. We want to bury each other, not make the other guy look good.

Ophelia and Ben wrestle a very funny David and Goliath match, a perfect choice for a 275-pound guy and a 120-pound girl. Ben plays the big lumbering hulk, and Ophelia, the small, clever woman who outfoxes him at every turn. She ducks under his clotheslines. She jumps over his spears. He tries to pick her up, and she wraps her legs around his neck and rides him as he staggers around blindly. He pretends to be a cad, gets angry, and tries to punch her. She circles behind him and kicks the back of his leg, taking him down. She slaps on the figure-four leglock. Ben hams it up, pretending to be in excruciating pain but refusing to tap out. "I can't submit to a . . . woman!" he moans.

"Try it, honey. You'll like it!" Ophelia growls, as Ben pounds both hands on the canvas.

We all laugh and spontaneously applaud. It was as good as a TV match.

"Well, well, well." Rat Boy is frantically making notes. "This is going to be a competition, after all. Okay, hotshots." He turns to me and Danny. "You're gonna have your hands full topping that."

"Okay," Danny begins as we huddle. "Let's do a slow-paced, technical—"

"No way! That's what you do best. I need to get some high spots in there and show what I can do."

"Okay, you can have your spots if I can win the match."

I hesitate. That might be okay, but would Rat Boy be subtly influenced by the outcome? In a close competition, wouldn't the winner have to look better than the loser?

"Are you guys writing the Declaration of Independence or booking a match?" Rat Boy yells. "Let's go!"

"Take your pick, Kyle. Your style or your outcome. You can't have both."

But I *want* it both ways. Still, I know if we wrestle his match—a bunch of holds and locks—I'll look like a little weakling. I have to risk the outcome and get my moves in there. "Okay, you win. You gonna finish with the shooting star?" He's so damn proud of his perfect shooting star press, a move I can't get to save my life.

"Yeah. I'll give you a DDT to set it up. Let's make it a cut-off match. You dominate for the first five minutes, then I'll take over. That way, we can each do our thing."

"Okay." I sure hope Rat Boy remembers my five minutes while he's enjoying Danny's five minutes.

"Are you designing costumes?" Rat Boy calls. "Composing entrance music?"

We rush through the rest of the booking and get in the ring. Danny swings at me. I duck and give him a perfect spinning heel kick. He staggers but doesn't go down! I'm screwed! It never occurred to me he'd be so low as to not sell my moves. I come back at him with a double dropkick. Same thing. He reels but keeps his feet. "You bastard," I mutter as he rushes by. I hear him laugh.

I hit him with an axe kick, an arm drag, and a hurricarana. Each time he springs up, fresh as a daisy. Bastard! *Well, just wait till it's his turn to show off. He'll put me in a front face lock and I'll whistle "Yankee Doodle." I swear I will.*

But then it occurs to me. Danny is screwing himself with this no-selling. If he keeps this up and I turn around and sell his moves, I look like the professional, and he looks like a brat. At least I hope so.

My part of the program comes to an end. I do my beautiful frog splash and Danny puts his knees up. I roll on the mat in fake pain. Danny looks surprised but he keeps going, dragging and tossing me like a rag doll for the next five minutes. I groan, I clutch my injured body parts, I cling to the ropes for support.

His shooting star lands a little off center, but I sell it like crazy, rolling out of the ring and onto the floor, curling up like a pill bug, coughing and panting. When I stand up, Rat Boy is watching me, not Danny. "I wondered if he was actually hurting you!" he cries with delight. "I swear to God I couldn't tell for sure. That was excellent, Kyle, just excellent. Sonny, you got yourself a spot. If you sell like that for me, you'll make me look great! Welcome to the pros!" He shakes my hand. Danny stands in the ring, seething. Forget the pros. I just hope I make it out of the showers alive today.

"You want to use your real name?" Rat Boy asks. "The show's only a month off. I have to get going on the publicity tonight."

"No, I want a handle. Let me think."

"Judas Iscariot!" Danny hisses from above.

"Bartleby the Scrivener!" Ophelia cries.

"Is that a dirty word?" Rat Boy asks her.

"No, it's perfect," I say. I spell it for him.

Rat Boy's phone rings. He runs to get it, and we all freeze while he talks. "Troy's gonna be fine," he tells us. "Just a reaction to the pills. They're going to keep him overnight for observation."

"Thank God!" says Ben.

"What's that? Oh, Kyle. He was awesome."

Jeff must have asked who won the tryout. Rat Boy holds the phone out to me. "How'd you do it?" Jeff asks me.

"He liked my selling," I tell him.

"Genius. He's picturing you selling to him. Very shrewd, Kyle." I try to enjoy this and not watch Danny stalking off to the showers.

Everyone else goes to change while Rat Boy gives me instructions. I'm going to wrestle him in the first match of next month's show at the Davie Rodeo Arena. "We're the curtain pullers, kid. The first match sets the tone for the whole show."

I nod and try to look professional as he talks, when inside I'm double-pumping and doing the happy dance.

"We'll be rehearsing here every Saturday until the show. You cannot be late, because I have a lot to teach you. Got it?"

"Yes, sir!"

"Okay, kid, don't drool on me."

While we go over everything, I see everyone else in the class leave the gym showered and dressed. But not Danny. Rat Boy notices, too. "You want me to go back to the locker room with you?"

"No," I say. "Don't I have to learn to handle this kind of stuff if I'm going to work in the pros?"

"Yeah, you do," he says. "Just don't mess up your pretty face before my show. Got it?"

"I'll try."

He picks up his gear and leaves, and I trudge off to my next fight.

Danny is showered and dressed, leaning up against a locker. When he sees me, he raises his hands and claps slowly—*clap, clap, clap*. I've never been sarcastically applauded before.

"Look, Dan. I just want to change and go home. Okay?"

"I just wanted to give you your props. You look so sweet and innocent, but you're the sharpest guy I've ever come up against."

"Danny, you did it to yourself. I didn't hypnotize you and tell you not to sell to me. When it was my turn I just did what I was supposed to do. If you do the same at the next tryout, you have a good chance of beating me. So why don't you go for that?"

"I know where I made my mistake. I didn't scout you right. But I've got you scouted now, and when you make a mistake, I'll be right there to take over."

"Good. I'm glad to know I have backup. Now, unless you get a kick out of watching other guys undress, could you leave?"

"Watch your back, Kyle. Fair warning."

"Thanks. And, hey, I'll see if I can get you a ticket to MY show."

He freezes in the doorway, but he gets control and walks on out. I know I shouldn't have said that last part. But I get so mad when people call me sweet.

Chapter 9

When I get home from work Thursday night, the TV is blaring again. It's Nickelodeon as usual, a rerun of *The Cosby Show*. I pause for a moment, since Lisa Bonet is on the screen, then wave to Chantal, who waggles her fingers at me. She's curled up with the dog, who looks contented, but I make my rounds anyway. First, I check Penelope's dishes for fresh food and water. Then I go through the trash to make sure Chantal didn't toss out any bills that need paying. Then I go through the mail and pull out any potential disasters. Chantal keeps getting us hooked into Time-Life books. They must call her during the day and she just says okay to whatever they suggest.

Everything seems to be okay today. For a second, I let my body sag against the kitchen wall. I think it's funny that on Monday, Wednesday, and Friday, when I spend two hours in wrestling class getting slung around and smashed into an unforgiving mat, I come home energized and fresh as a daisy. But on Tuesday, Thursday, and Saturday nights, when all I do is drive around delivering pizzas, I'm almost too tired to walk.

I casually check the rest of the house, making sure the stove is off, the refrigerator door is closed, no water is running, etc. Finally, I do the part I hate, I go back to Chantal's bedroom and rummage through her purse to make sure she has enough money and that she hasn't written any checks to any more weird charities. Then I count all her pills to make sure she took the right ones today. Everything is good today, except the clothes hamper is running over. I make a mental note to do some laundry over the weekend.

Then, back to the living room, where *The Fresh Prince* is coming on, heralded by its brain-pounding theme song. As Jeff would say, it's go time.

"Could we turn that off?" I call.

She cups her hand to her ear.

"Off? Can you turn that off? I need to talk to you."

She frowns at me. Apparently Will Smith means more to her than I do at this point, but she fishes in the couch cushions and digs out the remote. Beautiful silence fills the room. I think it's interesting that she has trouble doing so many things now, but she can operate the remote control perfectly.

"I have something important I want to tell you," I say, sitting down.

She winks at me. "Girl trouble?"

"Well, now that you mention it, I have two things to tell you. The first thing is that I have a girlfriend, and it's getting pretty serious."

"Are you being careful?"

The joys of a French grandmother. I feel myself blush. "Yes. Anyway, her name is Ophelia—"

"Rich gifts wax poor when the giver proves unkind."

"Uh, yeah. The thing is, she's a little older than me and—"

"Oh, my, my, my." She rubs one finger over the other, like naughty, naughty.

"Anyway, she and another friend of mine, Ben, will be coming to the ceremony next week."

Her eyes get that faraway look. "You're getting married? Next week?"

I get the familiar stab in the stomach when Chantal isn't tracking. "My high school graduation, Grandma."

"That's next week?"

"Sure. We talked about it yesterday."

"Are you sure?"

"Yes. It's a week from this Saturday."

"And do you want me to go?"

Ouch. "Yes, I do. Since you're the only real relative I have in this world!"

"Don't get upset . . . uhm . . ."

"Kyle!"

"Kyle. I just didn't know. I'll be happy to come to your—"

"Graduation."

"Yes." She starts inching her hand toward the remote.

"No, wait, there's something else I need to tell you." Now I'm more tired than ever. But I have to do this. "I know you were really happy about my final grades—"

"I was?"

"Yes! Don't you remember when they came last week? I had a three-point-eight average? My class rank was fifteen out of three hundred? You were thrilled."

She rubs her forehead. "I don't remember as well as I used to."

"I know." How in the heck do you rebel against someone who doesn't remember well enough to fight you? "It's okay, sweetie. You're eighty-six years old. You don't have to remember everything."

"I'm very proud of you," she says. "Even if I don't know what day it is."

"Well, wait, there's more. And you won't like this."

"Okay." She hasn't let go of the remote.

"I've decided I'm not going to college. I'm going to try and become a professional wrestler."

"A what?" Now she looks like the woman I know and love. Maybe I should have done more bad things over the years to keep her focused.

"A wrestler."

"Wrestler?"

"Yes."

"That's a profession? Wrestling?"

"It's a kind of performer, really. Like a professional acrobat."

"In the *circus*?"

"No. They give wrestling shows in every city in America. People who like wrestling come to see them. Some people just stay in one city, and some people, if they're good, travel around the circuit. And if you're really good, you get to work for Vince McMahon and be on TV."

"That fat man from Publisher's Clearing House?"

"No, Vince McMahon. Not Ed McMahon. Anyway, lots of people pay money to see wrestling."

"What kind of people?"

"All kinds of people. Little kids, a lot of men, even people your age come to the shows."

"They come to see acrobats pretending to wrestle with each other? Kyle, is this some kind of sexual thing?"

"No! It's an athletic thing! It's called sports entertainment. Meaning, it's like a sport, but it's all scripted like theater. You've seen me watching wrestling on Monday and Thursday nights—"

"Oh, that thing! Kyle, do you mean that terrible program where they hit each other with chairs? It's like The Three Stooges! Why would a boy like you with all your talent and brains want to do something foolish like that?"

These are some of the most complex sentences she's put together in weeks. Obviously, she needed stimulation. I've never actually thought about the answer to her question, but as soon as I hear it I know. "I want to be famous. And this is the only way I think I can do it. I'm a good gymnast, but I'm not good enough to make the Olympic team. I'm not good enough with words to write the great American novel. I'm not good enough in drama to be a Broadway star. But I'm good enough at all those things to have it add up to me being a really good wrestler. I've been taking lessons, and I'm the best one in my class. They want me to be in a show!"

"Your mother ran off to be a sculptress. Now you've found something even more foolish."

"Don't compare me to her! There's no comparison."

"But this is the same kind of thing. You'll always be chasing some kind of stupid dream, never having any real life for yourself—"

"It isn't the same kind of thing. Mom is a lousy artist. I'm a good wrestler. I've been in this school."

"School! How do you have a school for acting ridiculous?"

"It's hard for outsiders to understand, but it's very rigorous training. It's ten times harder than anything I ever did in gymnastics. You have to do really hard physical maneuvers, only you have to have perfect timing and work with a partner, almost like a trapeze artist—"

"Back in the circus again!"

"But it's like that. If you make a mistake you could injure or even kill your partner. And while you're doing all that, you have to act and play a role. You have to make speeches on the microphone. You have to create a character and make the audience either love him or hate him. Hardly anyone in the business can do all those things equally well. But my teacher says I've got the potential. I have a chance to make it in one of the most competitive fields there is. It's almost impossible to get into a show. But in just a few weeks, I've done it!"

"Ahhhh."

"What?"

"Now I see. You've always been like this, Kyle. You want to do things no one else can do. On the playground, as a little boy, you had to be the first to do everything. But if some other child figured out how to do the same thing, you would lose interest. You always had to be singled out, to be special."

I don't like hearing this, but since I know it's completely true, I don't deny it. "Why do you think I'm that way, Chantal?"

She looks like she knows the answer but doesn't want to give it.

"Tell me. I really want to know."

"Maybe it's all to get your mother to see she was wrong to leave you."

When something is really true, you hear it with your whole body. All the air rushes out of me at once, like Chantal has given me a body blow. "That's stupid, isn't it?" I say.

"Not if it spurs you to do things."

There's a long silence. "Will you come see me in my show?"

"Of course," she says. "I love you, no matter what kind of fool you turn out to be."

I get up and kiss her on the cheek. I have such a strong urge to cry I have to leave the room. When I come back later, she's immersed in *The Fresh Prince*, and her eyes have lost their focus again. I don't blame her. Sometimes clueless seems like the only way to be.

Fort Knocks is transformed every Saturday into a rehearsal hall for GCW, Gold Coast Wrestling. I walk in for my first rehearsal to find maybe a hundred people milling around. There are wrestlers working out in the ring, warming up, and practicing on the sidelines. There are technical guys messing with cables and sound equipment. There's a box of flyers by the door that say JUNE IS BUSTING HEADS ALL OVER. That must be the name of the show. There's a montage of wrestlers' pictures at the top (not mine), and then the card is listed. I'm right at the top, Bartleby the Scrivener vs. Rat Boy with Whisker-Biscuit. I guess I'll always remember my first match, a two-on-one handicap match with a rat in it.

The main event is a six-man street fight with several names I recognize. Jeff has explained to us that in the independent shows you see people on the way up to TV and people on the way down from TV. And you have to act like everyone's equal if you don't want your clock cleaned.

The only person in the room I know is Rat Boy, who is standing with two suits, all of them reviewing a clipboard. I walk up to them, even though they seem to be in the middle of a fight.

Rat Boy pounds his fist on the clipboard. "The TV spots made all the difference last month! Now you've made some money you want to get greedy with the overhead, and I can tell you the gate will drop ten percent if we don't get on TV. You think wrestling marks read the paper?"

Suit Number One says, "But now the target audience has found us, they'll be looking for the next show. Those TV spots are the biggest thing in your budget, man."

"Fine. You don't want to make money. Don't make money." Rat Boy sees me. "Oh, hey, Brian, Don. Here's the white meat I was telling you about. This is Kyle Bailey, Whisker-Biscuit's next willing victim."

One of the hardest things in wrestling is picking up all their slang expressions from context. I never heard "white meat" before, but I have to guess they aren't sizing me up for any pedophilic activity and that it's just another term for rookie. "How do you do?" I offer my hand to each of them.

"Don Brady is my partner and cofounder of GCW," Rat Boy says. "He's also our ring announcer, timekeeper, bell-ringer, and floor director. And this difficult guy who's acting like a cheapskate is our accountant and promotions manager, Brian Foster. His daughter opens every show with a really bad version of the national anthem."

"Hey!" says Brian as he shakes my hand.

"Jeff told me I have to prepare his students for the hardships of the show!" Rat Boy shoots back. "Listening to Chelsea sing is gonna be worse than any powerbomb he ever gets!"

I can see this is still about the advertising budget. "What do you want me to do?" I ask, in order to get away.

"Go change. I want to start laying out our match and let the rat get used to you."

"Okay." I make a quick retreat.

"Don't worry, kid!" Brian Foster yells after me. "If you can work with Rat Boy, you won't have any problems with vermin!"

My next challenge is the locker room, where two guys who look like they fell off Mount Olympus are having a private conversation. I know it's private because what I hear when I come through the door is, "I can get it for you, but you have to give me the money in advance."

Why do I always walk in on the damn drug deals? "Uh, hi," I say as they turn on me like two tigers. Danny and Troy have taught me a few things about locker room aggression, so I know to turn away, keep my eyes down, change my clothes, and mind my own business. The gymnastics team was never like this.

"Who in the hell are you?" asks my first new friend in professional wrestling. He is about six-foot-five and completely naked. I think I could deal with just bullies, but the concept of naked bullies is still giving me trouble.

"Kyle Bailey," I say, still keeping my head down.

Then I decide to take a risk. I turn around and extend my hand. "White meat."

Both of them crack up. "This must be the little child prodigy from the beginner's class. Jeff Broadhurst wants to marry you, kid!"

I laugh, since self-effacement is working so well. "I'm really excited to be in the show," I say. "And to work with guys like you." Now, mind you, I haven't a clue who these behemoths are, but I figure appealing to their massive egos is better than attacking their massive bodies.

One behemoth looks at the other. "He seems okay," he says, right out loud where I can hear him.

"Yeah, he's okay," says the other Neanderthal. "You didn't hear anything when you came in here, did you, kid?"

I know this answer. "Uh-UH!" I shake my head no for special emphasis.

"Yeah, he's okay. Change your clothes and beat it, Rat Bait. We're doing business in here."

"Yes, sir." I change quickly and scoot out the door, congratulating myself on passing this difficult test until I hear one of them say, "Keep an eye on him."

I wonder how many decades it takes until this little clan accepts you for real.

When I get back out, both my opponents, human

and rat, are waiting in the ring, and all the activity that was going on has stopped. Apparently, I am holding up rehearsal.

"What were you doing in there?" Rat Boy screams at me. "Getting a perm?"

I walk to the ring accompanied by raucous laughter. Note to self: Be early for everything in the future.

"All right, we're gonna lay out the whole show today," Rat Boy says to me. All the other wrestlers and employees are settling themselves in the bleachers or on the floor outside the ring. "Job one is we gotta make sure you can handle the rat gimmick. Some guys get the heebie-jeebies and ruin the bit. You're out cold, I take WB out of his cage and drop him on you. He's trained to crawl all over you, giving the audience what we like to call the *eeeew* factor. So let's see if you can lie still. Go down."

Maybe Chantal was right. Maybe I should go to college. But for now, I do my job, lie on my back and close my eyes. I hear the squeak of the cage door, then feel rat impact to my midsection. Rat Boy wasn't kidding when he said he would *drop* the rat on me. Rats are heavier than you think, or maybe this rat takes steroids. Anyway, I struggle to lie still while processing a series of nauseating sensations—little claws scraping my chest and arms, wiry whiskers in my face, a strong smell of something like cabbage and old closets and, worst of all, the long tail dragging over me. The tail feels longer than the rat. It's covered in some kind of tough skin that feels like scar tissue. When he gets close to my face I can hear his little puffy breaths. Also, everyone on the sidelines is participating by yelling "eeew" to try and rattle me. "Oh, God, he's going to shit on the kid!" calls out one wag, but that doesn't happen. I know Whisker-Biscuit is a trained professional. And so am I. I never move a muscle.

"Okay, excellent!" Rat Boy says. "While that's going on, I'm posting on the four corners, getting my big pop from the adoring crowd. It's very important for you to not move or upstage me in any way during this time." Finally he scoops up the rat. "Then I'll pick up my partner and put him in the cage. Don't move yet. In fact you need to stay out until I'm out of the ring, down the ramp, and out of sight. That means you count one potato, two potato, all the way to ten before you even stir. Then sit up. Do it now, look groggy and slightly nauseated."

No trouble there. I sit up and open my eyes, wiping off my face with my arm where my little opponent walked on me.

"Good, that's good, Kyle. Now you get up very slowly and slide out of the ring like you're on your last legs—

very good—and stagger a little. Cough, like you've inhaled lots of rat cooties. Sell it, come this way. All the way to the curtains, keep selling, great! That's great."

I'm at the "curtains," a space six feet from the locker room door, marked on the floor with freezer tape and a sign. Everyone is applauding me. Okay, it was worth having a rat walk on me.

"Great job, Kyle. Okay, come on back to the ring, and we'll lay out the match."

As I walk back, a few people give me a little pat on the shoulders. I don't really think what I did was a big deal, but I have picked up that if you suck up the things you don't like, you get respect. That's something I've been doing all my life.

Twelve hours later, the main event guys are rehearsing. It's unbelievable the level they have to work at, the timing, keeping track of five other guys, putting props in the right positions at the right times. The routine I worked out with Rat Boy was like doing the Hokey Pokey in kindergarten. These guys are doing high-speed ballet. And any mistake they make obviously breaks their necks, since they are sailing through the air, sometimes with another guy in their arms, and smashing each other with chairs, sticks, and garbage can lids. They go through the combinations again and again, some of them getting bruised and bloody in the process. I study everything they do, lose all track of time, so much that I don't even realize Rat Boy is sitting next to me on the bleachers.

"It's eight o'clock," he says to me. "You never even took a break to eat anything. Don't you want to go home?"

I look up at the high gym windows, surprised to see darkness. I missed my shift at work tonight. I'll probably get fired. And the thing is, I couldn't care less. "I think I AM home," I tell him.

He laughs and gives me a pat. "Another young life down the drain." He sighs. "Oh, well, it pays the bills. Hey!" he sees something he doesn't like in the ring and runs up to correct it.

They don't finish rehearsing till midnight. I leave with the last guys, bumming a ride, since the buses have stopped running for the night. It isn't till Sunday morning that I realize I also had a date with Ophelia and stood her up. That I do care about.

Chapter 10

Nobody thinks to throw me a graduation party, so I throw one for myself. I decided not to go to the actual ceremony—it was on a Saturday and I would have had to miss GCW rehearsal. Anyway, I feel like I've already left all those high school people behind. I have a whole new life.

"Which do you think is better, pizza or pasta?" Chantal asks Ben, her new best friend. We're at That's Amore under the big neon eel, eating two pizzas. One for Ben, one for the rest of us. Spaghetti and meatballs for Hector. I got to keep my job in exchange for having the party here and promising never to miss a shift again.

"Pizza, no contest," Ben says. "More saturated fat."

"Yes, exactly!" Chantal cuts her slice of pizza into delicate squares with her knife and fork. "Do you like

Greek food? I love the Greek culture. I love everything about it."

I'm baffled. All traces of the woman who forgets to feed the dog are gone. Maybe she needs to be around people more.

Ben puts two slices together, folds it all up like a taco, and takes a huge bite. "Who's your favorite character from Greek mythology?" he asks Chantal.

"Persephone. Her suffering made her more interesting than the other goddesses. You would pick one of the strong heroes, I would think. Hercules, perhaps?"

"Odysseus," Ben says. "I feel like my whole life is like that story. I keep trying to get somewhere, and I get sidetracked every time."

"I named our dog Penelope," Chantal says, "because when she was a puppy she was always unraveling my knitting."

She and Ben both laugh. Hector swivels to Ophelia and me for an explanation, but we just shrug. This is a side of Ben I've never seen either. I mean, we knew he worked in a library, but I didn't know he was this smart. I turn my attention to a different goddess, Ophelia the ice queen.

"Things will get better now," I tell her. "I just had too much on my plate when I was still in school. Now I just have wrestling class and rehearsal. And this job. Well, and I want to start going to a gym. And eventually get a day job that pays better. But—" I reach for her hand.

She snatches it away. "I remember now. You told me you broke up with your last girlfriend because she was too clingy and needy. I guess this is your MO. You pull away, the girl chases you, and then you can complain and feel superior. Well, you picked the wrong person this time, because I chase no one."

Hector stares at his spaghetti. He wants no part of either conversation.

I try to role model a nice low voice for Ophelia. "You don't understand. There's too much going on in my life. I can't juggle it all."

"Oh, God!" She tosses back her brassy, beautiful hair. "Maybe Danny was right about you. You've got a big head now because you've got a stupid slot in that GCW show. I suppose your life is just grueling now, picking out what tights to wear for your debut, practicing your autograph. . . ."

I don't need to hear Danny's name come out of her mouth. My secret fear is that Danny will take her away from me. I know he'd love to. "You just don't understand," I whine, feeling like a kid arguing with his babysitter about bedtime. How am I supposed to explain to her that I've had to supervise and care for the woman across the table who is now chatting about Proust and some girl named Madeline. No wait, it sounds like a madeleine is a cookie.

"It's going to get better now. You'll see," I say.

Ophelia gives a snort. "I think I'll have a glass of wine." She holds up her hand for the waiter.

"Oh, no you won't!" I say, grabbing at her hand. "We have an agreement."

"I don't think we really do." She yanks her hand away so violently, she knocks over our Pepsi pitcher, and it goes everywhere. I grab about a thousand napkins and go to work, while Ben and Chantal turn to stare at us.

Hector makes the save. "Why did they have to unmask the Dark Angel, anyway?" he says. "He was cool with the mask. Now he's just a bald guy."

The whole energy of the table shifts. All of us clamor to give our opinion of the Dark Angel's character and what direction it should take. Chantal turns her eyes to the window, staring out at the night.

It's magic time. Bartleby the Scrivener, dressed in red tights, black boots, and black knee pads—all hand-me-down gifts from Rat Boy—is standing in a rodeo locker room, shaking and trying to listen to the voices that are screaming all around him.

"I want you to walk out fast when you hear your name,

go straight to the ring, no posing or showing off. Then stand there quietly and don't upstage Rat Boy's entrance."

I wonder if throwing up would constitute upstaging someone.

"Hey, this kid is sweating like a pig! Somebody towel him off!"

"This is the jobber from the wrestling school? Is that what you're going to wear, kid?"

"Hey, did you guys see the house? It's packed out there! I told you those TV spots would do it. It's a hot crowd, too. They're out there chanting and yelling already."

"You hear that, kid? Your job is to not kill that nice hot crowd by being boring or blowing all your spots."

I can hear it. I think of the mob who set fire to Dr. Frankenstein's house.

"Those tights look kind of loose, don't they? They look like they're going to fall off him."

I didn't think it was possible, but I shake harder.

"Is the Walking Nightmare here? I haven't seen him all day."

"He better be here. He's up right after the Rat Boy segment."

"Hey! There's a fight breaking out in the ringside seats. Some guy in a wheelchair is hitting some woman with a program."

"Oh, jeez. I know who that is. He came last month. Just call the cops now, he talks back to our security."

"What's he hitting a woman for?"

"That's his wife."

"Listen, you guys. It's seven-twenty-five, and the natives are getting restless. Where's Chelsea?"

"Here, Daddy!"

"Honey, what are you doing in the men's locker room? Didn't I tell you about that before? Come on, let's get out there. Are you ready to sing for the people?"

"Yes!"

"What are you wearing, sweetheart? You look like a slut."

"Mommy said it was okay."

"Yeah, that figures. Okay, sweetie, stop looking at that man and let's get going. We've got a show to do."

I don't want to do this. I want to go to college and have a real job where I don't have to worry about throwing up or having my tights fall down. A job where no one will drop me on my head or throw a folding chair at me. Just as I'm about to head for the exit, two strong hands land on my shoulders. It's Rat Boy on one side of me and Jeff on the other.

"How's our little prodigy?" Rat Boy asks me. He's all dressed up in his moth-eaten outfit. "Have you been back here freaking yourself out? Because everyone does that the first time."

"And the second time," says Jeff. "And all the other times."

"Listen, junior. I want you nice and loose so you won't make a mistake and injure me or, worse, kill the crowd for my match. Remember, this is fun. It's a mad tea party. All those people out there are just a deck of cards."

"Jokers, mostly," says Jeff.

"And some queens!" adds Rat Boy.

I try to laugh, but it just comes out as a different kind of shaking.

"Listen," Jeff says. "Your whole class is out there rooting for you, plus some old lady."

"That's my grandmother."

"Kyle, you're trembling like a schoolgirl." Rat Boy is stretching now. In the distance I hear the crowd quiet down and something that sounds like a cross between a cat and a peacock singing the national anthem. "Knock it off. You aren't that important in this show. You're a nameless, faceless jobber to these people. They expect you to screw up. It doesn't matter what you do out there. It's like your first time having sex. It's just something you get out of the way, and then you start figuring out how to do it better. Okay?"

That helps. "Okay."

"That's my boy!" He claps me hard on the shoulder. "Listen, Jeff, if he passes out, wheel Granny into the ring. We'll finish the match with her."

This time I do laugh for real. The crowd gets loud again. I hear Don Brady welcoming the fans, telling them what a hot show we have, and threatening them with legal action if they tape anything or point lasers at us. He asks some kind of question that gets a huge response. Maybe if they're ready for the show. Then he switches to a different voice I can hear clearly. "Ladies and gentlemen, here is your first contest. Introducing, from parts unknown, weighing in at one hundred fifty-four pounds, Barnaby the Scribbler!"

Note to self: Next time pick a handle every announcer can understand. I feel a gentle shove and start walking. We have a weird entrance route at the rodeo arena. The dressing area is in a separate building from the arena, since horses and bulls don't get dressed. So we exit the locker room and walk under the bleachers to a section where they've set up a tunnel of black cardboard with black curtains. I look up through the bleachers at the hundreds of asses and feet of the fans, smelling the circus smell of a wrestling show—overcooked hot dogs, spilled beer, burned sugar, and human sweat. I step through the curtains. The crowd starts in right away. "Who are you? Who are you?" I know from experience as a fan, it could be worse. I follow my instructions and walk across the sand between the bleachers and the "ringside seats." Ten rows of folding chairs. A little kid stretches his hand out to me. I try not to break down and cry as I slap his hand. I'm officially a babyface, which means I'm allowed to be nice to fans. Heels have to treat them badly. The chanting switches to "Rat Bait! Rat Bait!" as I climb up the steps and get in the ring. I don't hit myself with the ropes. I don't throw up. My tights don't fall down. I lean back against the ropes for a moment of relaxation. The ring looks different at night with klieg lights shining on it, sort of like a firelit cave. There are about a million moths flying around. The referee, David Allen, gives me a reassuring smile. Don raises the mic again. "And his opponent, from Pembroke Pines, Florida, weighing one hundred seventy-two pounds and accompanied by his special friend, Whisker-Biscuit—Rrrrrrrat Boy!"

The fans jump up and fill the air with their roars, screams, claps. Rat Boy is officially a heel, but a lot of the fans like him anyway. He tries to deflect their love as he stalks out by giving them the finger and threatening them with his rat. I use the time to find my "family" in the bleachers. Chantal looks a little lost. The others catch my eye and go wild, jumping up and down and pointing at me. All except Danny, who keeps his arms folded. What a guy.

Rat Boy slides into the ring and shows me the rat cage. Then he puts it on the apron for safekeeping. The bell rings, and we move into a collar and elbow tie-up. I try to think several moves ahead to make sure I know what I'm doing, but that throws me off and I stumble a little.

The crowd picks up on it. "You fucked up! You fucked up!"

"Concentrate!" hisses Rat Boy. "Get your head out of your ass."

My adrenaline rushes, and my brain clears up. Rat Boy drops me with a clothesline, and I go down perfectly. I stagger up and into a punch. Then he throws me into a side headlock. "Rat Bait! Rat Bait! Rat Bait!" screams the crowd.

"That's the stuff," he whispers in my ear.

The referee kneels down and asks me if I want to quit. I shake my head bravely, all the while screaming in pain. The crowd starts clapping and pounding their feet, to encourage me. I'm touched. Fulfilling their expectations, I struggle to my feet and break the head-lock with three elbows to Rat Boy's midsection. Then I swing at him and miss, and he picks me up and suplexes me. I make a satisfying crash to the mat. For the next five minutes, Rat Boy tosses me around like a rag doll. This is the hardest part of the match because the rag doll is the one who does all the work. I have to keep remembering what's coming next and how to land. He picks me up for an airplane spin, not my best maneuver. I land on my back great, but I screw up sometimes when I have to fall on my face. I want to put my hands down and catch myself. I try closing my eyes while he spins me around, and it works better. I make a perfect landing.

We're in the homestretch now. I get two seconds to show off and impress the crowd. Which means I put a dropkick and a frog splash on Rat Boy and roll him up fast for what looks like it might be an upset. It's only a two-count of course, but naturally it makes Rat Boy very angry. His acting is so good it kind of scares me as he grabs the scruff of my neck and walks me to the turnbuckle, where he smashes my head into the padding several times while the audience counts. I fall down. He picks me up and gives me a DDT, making it look like he's snapped my neck for sure. I fall again. The crowd senses the finish of the match and starts screaming "Rat Bait! Rat Bait!" again. I lie still, panting, exhausted, thrilled. My work is over. I did good.

"Ratify him! Ratify him!"

I hear the squeak of the cage door and Old Cabbage Breath drops on my chest, milling around and dragging his tail right across my face, which draws squeals of horror from the happy crowd. I remember to lie still as Rat Boy poses on all four corners. Finally he picks the damn rat off me. I listen to the cheers continue as Rat Boy makes his exit. Finally I sit up, coughing and spitting out rat cooties. I hear the audience laugh as I struggle to my feet, slip out through the ropes and stagger toward the curtains. Several people brush hands with me as I walk by. I already have fans. "You suck, Bartleby!" yells a voice that's unmistakably Danny. Since he's playing the game I can't be mad, but I know he means it. I don't care. He's in the bleachers. I'm walking through the curtain.

On the other side, Jeff and Rat Boy swoop in on me and practically pick me up and twirl me around. "You were great!" Jeff says. "I can't believe how great you were! Didn't I tell you, Rat Boy? Didn't I tell you? This is the best first-year guy I've ever had."

"You're a natural, Kyle," Rat Boy tells me. "You just froze for a second at the beginning, and after that you were in the flow. If you want a job in the July show, you got it."

They walk me back to the locker area, talking back and forth about every aspect of my performance and how wonderful it was.

"Okay, Kyle, shower and change," Rat Boy says. "Put on this GCW T-shirt and get down to the merchandise table. The fun part of your job is over for tonight."

Two hours later, I've sold about fifty T-shirts, two championship belt replicas, and about a hundred autographed pictures and packs of trading cards. I've had my picture taken with a lot of little boys, several teenage girls, and one older couple. Oh, and I have a fan club. Six guys from Silver Trail Middle School. One of them was the kid who slapped my hand. They've completely lost the thread of the show in their pursuit of me. They only leave my table to go to their parents for more souvenir money. Don Brady comes by at one point, looks in the till, and smiles at me.

Ophelia brings me a Coke. "How's Chantal doing?" I ask.

"Pretty well," she says. "I don't think this is her kind of show. She went to the bathroom and took an awful long time, but I guess it was okay."

"You didn't take her?" I scream. "What were you thinking?"

"What's your problem? She's not a child. You really act kind of overprotective sometimes."

"She could get lost or confused."

"Kyle, she's a very intelligent, vibrant woman. Just because she's older doesn't mean—"

"Who lives with her, you or me?"

"You're such a damn control freak!"

Luckily, this romantic interlude is interrupted by the return of my fan club with still more money. "We want an autographed picture of you!" says Carlos, their leader.

"Oh, sorry, buddy, I'm new here. I'm not cool enough to have merchandise on the table yet."

They all stand there, looking like Christmas was canceled. Then Carlos notices Ophelia. "Is this your girlfriend?"

I look at her nervously. "I hope so." Which makes her laugh.

"Man!" says Carlos. "Man!"

"I'm a wrestler, too," Ophelia tells him. "You wanna take a picture with me?"

I get to hold the camera. "No touching!" I have to repeat this several times.

"Can you autograph somebody else's picture for us?" asks Carlos's sidekick, Andrew.

"Well, they didn't cover that in my training, but I don't think I better do that. Tell you what. Bring me your programs, and I'll autograph those for you, okay?"

"Okay!" They race off.

I turn my attention back to the ring, where the main event is going down. When I see a six-man street fight performed by really great wrestlers, I realize what I did in the ring was nothing. It's like watching a symphony orchestra perform without a conductor and with headphones to block out the sound. Yet they all stay together. I'm getting completely lost in it when I hear Ophelia scream out my name. Even before I turn around, I get a terrible feeling in my stomach. Then I turn and see Chantal slumped in Ben's arms, unconscious. I thought I would get through the night without throwing up, but I was wrong.

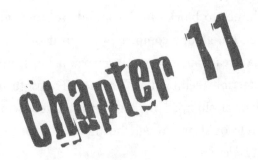

Chapter 11

My next match takes place underwater. They've flooded the whole arena—it seems to be Madison Square Garden—and fixed it so that somehow all of us can breathe. My opponent is all in black and wears a mask. He's way bigger than me. I see the flash of his teeth as he laughs at me. Huge streams of bubbles come from the announcer's mouth, then the fans start cheering and a tidal wave of bubbles hits me, almost knocking me over. The bell rings and we surge toward each other.

I try to grab my opponent and overestimate, sailing above his head. I realize that without my full weight, I have no power at all. We both struggle to take each other down, but our feet fly up instead as we roll around helplessly in our own wakes. Then my opponent grabs me in a chokehold, which I realize too late is the right move for underwater. I gesture frantically to the ref as the bubbles pour out of me, and I clearly think, *I'm going to die.* In desperation, I reach up and claw at the mask. Sometimes, according to the weird laws of wrestling, if you unmask an opponent, he will give up and run away. My body gets weaker, but I feel the material give under my fingers. I use my last ounce of strength to rip the mask away.

I scream. It's Chantal, and her eyes are cloudy and weird, like a blind person or a fish. She floats toward me, and I try to back away, but my feet fly up and she grabs my ankle. I know she's going to kill me, and I start to cry.

"Are you all right?" A nurse is touching my shoulder. It's Caroline. I remember her from the first shift yesterday. She comes at seven and leaves at three.

I look immediately to Chantal in her jacked-up ICU bed, looking small and pale. She's still asleep, breathing hard. Her skin is pale, bluish. I look at her monitor. Her blood pressure is 190 over 121. Her pulse is ninety-six. The little jaggedy line is rolling along, and the beeps are normal and steady. She collapsed Friday night. It's Sunday morning now, and still no one has told me what happened, what's wrong with her. They just keep testing, wheeling her off for this and that, stuff I'll bet anything her Medicare HMO isn't going to cover.

I'm still crying, and Caroline doesn't wait for my answer. I'm not the patient, after all. She checks all the tubes going into and out of my grandmother, adds a bag, takes away a bag. It's scary to think that that's all we are—something fluids go in and out of.

"I was having a bad dream," I say, blowing my nose. "How is she?" Even though I can read the monitors for myself.

Caroline repositions Chantal, adjusting her as if she were a doll. "She's holding her own. Did she sleep through the night?"

"She woke up once and said she was in pain. They gave her something."

"Are you going home? You should grab a shower before rounds."

This is the litany I've been hearing since Friday night. Everyone wants me to go home and take a shower. Maybe I stink. The last thing I did before this happened was wrestle a guy and have a rat walk on me. I look pretty stupid, still in Rat Boy's tights, covered by a sweatshirt Ben gave me that swims on me.

"I'm okay," I say. "I want to stay here, if I can."

"You can." She smiles at me. "But you're allowed to take a break. We're taking care of her."

I don't disagree with her. I mean, yes, they're keeping her alive and checking her vitals and stuff. But there are little things, like if she gets a pain, she doesn't call them, she just winces, so I have to be alert for that. Or if she slides off the pillow and her neck gets in a bad position, they might not notice for hours.

Caroline waters Chantal's only bouquet—a bunch of roses from Gold Coast Wrestling—and goes off to the next room.

I crawl out of my recliner and stretch. Chantal's room is in a corner of the building with two windows. Pink sunrise light is coming in from two angles. It's so pretty, like the inside of a seashell or that nail polish Ophelia wears. I go to the window and just stare at the light, like a thirsty person drinking water.

My vision is a little blurry at this point, and I have a really bad headache. I know I need to eat. I don't have any money, though. My gym bag is still back in my locker at the rodeo arena. I know Chantal's purse is in the closet, but I don't want to go into it somehow, when she's like this. It would feel like stealing.

I wonder if I should call my mother. She has a right to know her mother collapsed, but I'm afraid to call. I guess I'm scared she'll act like I bothered her and that will make me smash the hospital phone to smithereens, something definitely not covered by Chantal's health insurance.

"What's going on?" Chantal wails from the bed. She

talks in this faint, whiny voice, nothing like her real voice.

"You're in the hospital, Grandma. You fainted. Remember?"

"The hospital!" she says, as if I must be lying.

I come to her side and clutch the bedrails. I'm a little wobbly on my feet. "Sit back. You're in Coral Springs Medical Center. Remember we came in here Friday night? Now it's Sunday morning."

She shakes her head. "I don't remember anything." Her hands fidget around like something is bothering her. I wish I could read her mind.

"I'll be right back," I tell her. The nurses like to know when the patient wakes up.

Caroline is apparently with another ICU patient. There's a woman I don't know at the central desk, typing on the computer. "My grandmother's awake," I tell her.

She looks at me. "So?"

I guess they can't all be like Caroline. "Caroline asked me to tell her."

"Caroline is busy right now."

I sway a little. I think about asking her for money for the cafeteria. "I know that, but could you tell her when she gets back—"

"You can tell her."

"I won't know when she comes back!" I point to Chantal's room. "I can't see through the walls!"

She finally stops tapping computer keys and looks at me. "Why don't you go home and take a shower?"

My knees buckle, and I grab the desk. I see a mirage coming down the hallway toward us. It looks like Ophelia in a white sleeveless dress, carrying a McDonald's bag and paper cup of coffee, my gym bag slung over her shoulder. Then the urge to cry returns. She's *real*.

"I got sick of waiting for you to call and tell me what you need," she says. "So I just brought you what I thought you might need."

I can smell the grease. I can smell the melted cheese, egg, bacon. "God bless you!" I practically sob.

"Go down to the visitor's lounge with that," says Florence Nightingale.

Ophelia watches me cram food into my mouth with her mouth open. "Haven't you eaten anything since Friday night?"

"Friday noon," I say around a mouthful of cinnamon roll. I swallow and drink some coffee. It's so wonderful. Foods and beverages are so wonderful. "Rat Boy told me not to eat before a match."

"That's thirty hours ago!" she scolds. "What is wrong with you, Kyle? Are you some kind of martyr? Look, when you finish this, go home and take a shower. I'll stay with Chantal if you're afraid to leave her alone here in intensive care."

"I know it sounds obsessive, but they miss all kinds of stuff. When she's in pain she doesn't use the call button. She tells me."

"Well, maybe if you weren't there, she'd learn to use the call button."

"Or maybe she'd just lie there and suffer. Jeez, what is wrong with you?"

"What's wrong with you? I'm your girlfriend. You haven't even bothered to call me since I saw you leave the arena, thirty hours ago, in an ambulance! Didn't you think I'd want to know how Chantal is? Or how you are?"

"I had more important things on my mind!"

She sits back, blows out a breath, which I know is her technique for controlling anger. "You don't get it, do you? Well, anyway, I'm here. Go home and clean up. Take a little nap. Ben went to church this morning, but he said he could come this afternoon. And Jeff is bringing you a surprise tonight."

"I'm really not in the mood for surprises."

She smiles mysteriously. "You'll *get* in the mood for this one. Are you going or not? I'll sit right there and watch Chantal every second. I promise. Go."

I'm scared to go. I'm scared that if I leave Chantal, she'll die. Okay, I am messed up. I do need some sleep.

"All right, you win." I finish my coffee in one gulp.

"That's my boy." She fishes in her purse and gets out her car keys. "I'm in the front lot, by the front door."

I stand up on my spaghetti legs. "All right, but listen. When she's in pain she won't say so. She just scrunches her face a little. You have to ask her what's wrong. And her pillow works its way under her neck and makes her uncomfortable. She might want the TV on, but then again—"

She grabs my arm and Irish-whips me through the doorway. "Go!"

Penelope has peed all over the rug. Her food and water dishes are empty, and she gives me a look when I come in the door like, *Hello, traitor.* I had totally forgotten she existed until the moment I saw her. "Now you know how my girlfriend feels," I tell her. I feed her, walk her, and clean the rug. I bring in Friday and Saturday's mail and sort through that, making sure there are no problems with bills or anything. I shower and change into normal clothes. I realize I didn't want to take off my wrestling clothes. Everything was so wonderful Friday night and now . . . By then it's nine-fifteen. I stand by the phone for a long time, reciting my mother's phone number to myself. It's funny I know it by heart, since I've probably only used it ten times in my life. But I never pick up the receiver. I want to get out of the house. All the lights and shadows look creepy, and I can't stand the sound of Penelope's nails on the kitchen floor.

"Hello, Chantal! How are you doing today?" Dr. Sloane flips through the chart. He's one of those loud, overly cheerful doctors.

"I don't know." She tries to shift in the bed and winces. "I must have fallen down." She looks better than when I left. There's color in her face, and someone, either Caroline or Ophelia, has fixed her hair.

"No, you didn't fall down, Chantal. We think you've been having what we call transient ischemic attacks." He turns to me. "Small strokes that affect the brain. Have you noticed a change in her memory lately? Or just her functioning in general?"

"Yes." It's a relief that someone agrees with me. Everyone telling me how sharp and vibrant she was made me think I was going crazy. Still, the idea of her having "little strokes" is more than I can process at the moment. "What are you going to do for her?"

"I'm going to have a neurosurgeon come in and give her some cognitive tests. That will tell us a lot about her ability to carry on her activites of daily living. Does she live alone?"

"No. She lives with me."

"Well, we'll probably have some recommendations

for you. For now, I want to put her on blood thinners and vitamin E. That may help a bit, but as she has more and more of these . . . events, her function may continue to decline."

I look at Chantal to see if she's understanding this. She's fishing around in the bed. Probably looking for the remote.

"The sad part is," says Dr. Sloane, as he marks and flips the chart, "if she had Alzheimer's, there would be some therapies we could try. With this kind of vascular dementia, there's usually nothing we can do."

I don't answer him or say good-bye. I just let all the words tumble around in my brain. *Strokes, attacks, dementia, decline.*

"I'm glad you got rid of that salesman, Dennis," Chantal says to me.

Dennis? Who's Dennis? Then I remember that's my grandfather's name. "I'm Kyle, Grandma. You know that."

"Kyle?" she says.

"Your grandson. Get some rest, okay? Everything is going to be fine."

She smiles at me. "Really?"

When Ben comes in the afternoon, we work out a schedule. Ophelia will spell me in the mornings before she goes to work, and Ben will come after work in the afternoons. That way I can keep up with Penelope and whatever emergencies might happen at home. After I talk to Ben in the visitor's lounge, we go in to see Chantal.

"Oh!" She struggles to sit up. "What does *he* want?"

"It's me, Ben, Mrs. Bailey. Remember that nice dinner we had? We talked about Proust and—"

"Dennis! Who is this black man? Get him out of here!"

Embarrassment scalds my face. "She's confused, Ben. It's . . . I think it's the medication she's on."

He backs up. "It's okay, Dennis," he says, obviously trying to joke us back to a comfortable place. "My face would scare anybody."

"I hope no one else comes by!" Chantal says when he's gone.

Jeff and Rat Boy find me in the cafeteria eating my dinner. A hospital cafeteria is usually a fairly quiet place, since you have exhausted health care workers and upset family members, but Jeff and Rat Boy liven up the mood right away.

"Here's the little showstopper!" Rat Boy calls from the doorway. He's waving a newspaper. "Wait till you see this!"

They plunk down on either side of me, and Jeff actually pulls my food away so they can put the paper in front of me. It's a captioned photo by Derry Wilcox, who writes the local wrestling column for the *Sun-Sentinel*.

Usually he just has this column on Friday, summing up what the WWE is doing and giving ticket information for them and then for us smaller promotions. But this is in the entertainment section of the Sunday paper. The picture is what I see first. It's me, upside down in the air, being suplexed by Rat Boy. My form, I have to note, is just about perfect.

GCW COMES OF AGE

Industry mavens say the future of wrestling lies with the independent promotions who constantly bring in fresh talent and work without the constraints of television. GCW's most recent show, *June Is Busting Heads All Over*, presented at the Davie Rodeo Arena last Friday night, illustrated this point to perfection. The show had everything, and everything was well done. From the opening bout between gimmicky GCW owner Rat Boy (Dylan Pike) and some kid from a local wrestling school who had the look of a young Jason Quest, to the main event featuring Jon Strickland, among others, this show offered all the athleticism, drama, and crowd-pleasing hoopla any fan could hope for. With shows like this, Vince McMahon had better look over his shoulder. Tickets are on sale now for the July Fourth GCW extravaganza. Hooray for the Red, Black and Blue.

I'm breathing hard. Jason Quest is my idol. Jeff claps me on the back. "There you are, Kyle. You're 'some kid'!

You look like a young Jason Quest! You got ink on your very first time out!"

"You can't buy advertising like this!" Rat Boy explains, stuffing my French fries into his mouth. "The phones started ringing this morning with orders for the July show. I want to move you up the card a little, maybe have you job to the Killing Machine. If that goes okay, I'd really like to offer you a contract. If there's a young Jason Quest around here, I want him in my organization."

Jeff looks like a proud father. "I kept telling everyone you were the best new student I ever had. The best. Only six months of training and you can impress a reporter like that? It's unheard of. In fact, you'll have to be extra nice to everyone else in the locker room so they won't resent you."

"Yeah." Rat Boy chuckles. "Like the five major stars that were listed as 'among others.'"

"We need to step up your training," Jeff says, as my head swivels again. I feel like a tennis ball. "I was about to promote you to the intermediate class anyway, but now I want you to skip that and go right to the advanced. I think you need that, and you're ready for it. It's going to be a lot of work."

I swivel again. "I want to change your handle to Some Kid," Rat Boy says. "I got the idea from this article. Because that's what you are now. Some kid out of nowhere taking the world by storm. The fans will love that. So what do you say?"

I keep looking back and forth, then I look down at the paper. I can't believe that's a picture of me. But it is. "Can I give you my answer next week?" I say softly.

"Next week!" Rat Boy shouts so loud everyone turns to look at him. "What is this? Did you get an agent already? Jeff, does he get this? Does he appreciate what's going on here?"

Jeff touches my arm. "You can't hesitate, Kyle. Rat Boy has to capitalize on this right now, while people remember the article. You'll have to train all four weeks to be ready for the kind of match he wants to put you in. This is no time to ask for a vacation."

I stare at the picture and then at both of them. It's like a dream or something. It isn't real. "I don't think I can do it," I say.

Chapter 12

I was four when my mother dropped me off at Chantal's. I thought it was just for a visit because neither of them said anything. Since I liked my grandmother's house better than my mother's, I didn't ask any questions. But finally, after a few weeks, I guess some natural thing kicked in, and I remember saying to Chantal, "When is Mommy coming back?"

I remember every detail. We were sitting in some kind of cafeteria or soda fountain. I had a turkey sandwich with mustard on it and a vanilla shake. Chantal had gotten me excited about vanilla. She loved it, and she said any fool could appreciate chocolate, but people with a real sense of taste understood the subtlety of vanilla. She told me it was made from orchids, which for some reason just totally captivated me. I had the weird combination of vanilla and mustard in my mouth when she stirred her shake with her straw and said, "I don't know, Kyle. Maybe never."

Never. The word went down through my body, turning over and over, like a sinking stone. Even at four, I didn't like my mother. She was always too busy, making me feel like I was this big interruption in her important life. She never hugged me or touched me like Chantal did, never knew what things I liked, never noticed how I was feeling. I remember once standing in front of her, crying, and she just said, "Knock it off. That won't work." Chantal, on the other hand, was always smiling at me and saying things like, "I could eat you up with a spoon."

I knew all that, but my mother was still my mother. Chantal could just as well have said to me, "I'm sorry, but you'll have to grow up without a face." I never ate mustard or vanilla again.

I need to run. I'm up to ten miles a day now. My biggest fear, besides Chantal dying, is that I'll get fat now that I'm not as active as I was. Cooped up in the house all day, you think about food a lot. If it's a day when Chantal doesn't feel like eating, I find myself eating more, like that will make up for it. I've probably lost muscle in the past two months, too. Running doesn't work enough muscle groups, but I just don't want to go to the gym. It's too much like what I left behind.

Something about running stirs up all these old memories, too. Or maybe I'm just remembering because now I'm doing the same things for Chantal that she used to do for me. I coax her into telling me what she'd like for breakfast. I help her get dressed and make sure her shoes are on the right feet and her blouse is buttoned up the right way. I find a TV program I think she'll like for at least an hour. Then I grab the dog, lock the house, and go running.

Today we're going past the city playground. Penelope likes the other way, where we go by some woods and she can smell other animals' trails, but I like the playground. Now that it's summer, you can see all the little kids playing basketball and whatever, having dreams. Having everything in front of them.

I get winded right by the playground fence and stop and rest with my hands on my knees. The kids stare at me. Maybe I look like stranger danger to them. I was thinking maybe I could go on in there someday and coach them a little, but I can see from their faces they want me and my dog to move on.

I walk for a while, trying to enjoy the scenery, but then I start picturing which bills need paying and how I have to get Chantal a doctor's appointment, and I have an ongoing battle with her life insurance company. She let her policy lapse before I took over the bills, and they give you a very hard time about reinstatement. In general, we have no problems about money. We always lived on Chantal's income. Her checks go even farther now, because we never go anywhere.

Penelope wants to stop, so I wait while she sniffs around and decides if this clump of grass is the perfect place to pee. I try to force my mind to something good, like Ophelia. She's still my girlfriend, for reasons I don't fully understand. Sometimes when I need to go out and run errands, she watches Chantal for me. I'm scared to spend the night at her place, and I feel weird having sex at my house, because I don't want Chantal to walk in on us. Most of the time, we end up having sex in her car, parked in my garage. We never go out or do anything fun, because I have a one-hour time limit before I start picturing Chantal lying on the floor.

Penelope finally pees and when she's done I urge her to run some more. Running lets my anger out, lets me pound concrete with my feet. Sometimes I like to run until my chest hurts so bad I think I'm having a heart attack.

Jeff makes some stupid attempt about every week to get me back into wrestling. He doesn't get it. He has a wife taking care of his kids when he goes out to work.

Chantal needs something almost every minute. Her balance is terrible, and she falls a lot, even when she's using a cane or a walker. Older people really can't get up when they fall. That commercial is no joke. She doesn't call for help either, which I think is so weird. She just lies there and waits for me to find her. So I have to pay attention.

Anyway, Jeff called me last week saying they found a watch in the locker room and it looked like mine. I know he thinks if I get back into the gym and smell the sweaty canvas, I'll get hooked again. I told him I had my watch on and was looking right at it. He's not so bright. He should have said it was a sweatshirt or something.

I realize I'm running so fast I'm almost dragging Penelope. I slow down a little.

Rat Boy is the opposite. When I refused his offer to be in the July show, he cut me dead. He didn't even send me an e-mail, thanking me for doing a great job in June or anything. He hired Danny on the spot. Danny wrestled in the July and August shows, doing the rat bit. Ophelia tells me that this month, in the Fall from Grace show, he's moving up the card, just like I was going to. He has a singles match with Gluteous Maximus. Well, good luck with that. The guy weighs three hundred pounds, and his gimmick is he sits on your face. Ophelia and Ben have moved up to the intermediate class, and Troy is now in the advanced class, although he hasn't been in a show yet. I think they're watching him to make sure he doesn't abuse supplements again.

Penelope sees our house and collapses in the yard. I lie down next to her, and both of us stare up at the sky, gasping for air.

Chantal wants frozen waffles for lunch. I let her eat anything she wants, because she's so thin. I'm cutting them into little squares when the phone rings.

"Hey, champ! How's the caretaker business?"

"Hi, Jeff, what do you want?"

"I need your help, buddy. I've got a problem down here, and I think you could solve it."

I put the knife and fork down so I can focus my full attention on being angry. "Jeff, for Christ's sake! There's a hundred guys who want to be in wrestling! Move on. I mean, I'm really flattered but—"

"There are not a hundred guys with your ability."

I take a deep breath. "Like I said, I'm really flattered, but what you don't understand is that I have a responsibility here, and I can't just run around doing fun stuff."

"Ophelia was telling me you could get help. They have some daytime programs in Broward County, or maybe a visiting nurse, just enough so you could come back to class, go to the gym, maybe even work a show—"

"And then what! A scout sees me from the WWE, I get asked to move to Ohio for training, and eventually I'd have to travel two hundred and sixty days out of the year. Where does that leave my grandmother? I'll tell you where. In a goddamn nursing home!" Yikes. I didn't mean to get that loud. I look around the corner into the living room, but Chantal is immersed in *Sanford and Son*.

"All right. Look, Kyle, I can't tell you what to do with your life."

"Thank you!"

"But today, I really need your help. Hector is really stuck, really blocked, and I can't get through to him. He always worked well with you and respected you. I think maybe you could get him over this wall."

"Shit."

"Come again?"

"You heard me. I said shit. Because for weeks and weeks you've been poking around trying to figure out which of my buttons to push—envy over Danny, power and glory, lost watches. And now I guess you figure I'm a puppet for anyone who needs me, and I said shit because it's true. And now I'll feel bad if I don't come down there and help poor old Hector."

"Good," says Jeff. "But not because I'm trying to control you. I really do need your help."

"Yeah, fine. You've been training wrestlers for ten

years, and I've got the key to what you need to do. Okay. I'll see you at three."

"Great. And Kyle, I'm really grateful to you. You don't even know."

"Save it." Gratitude is the other thing that hooks me.

I bring Chantal her tray with the waffles and a side dish of applesauce. I put cinnamon on it, like she used to do for me.

"Oh, this is so nice!" she says. "Thank you!"

"Do you mind if Ophelia comes to stay with you for a couple of hours this afternoon? I have to go out."

"Ophelia," she says. "The pretty girl?"

"Right. I need to go out for a couple of hours, and she's going to stay with you."

She frowns. "That's today?"

"Yes." I'm used to this. She'll get it eventually.

"Okay. Kyle, could I please have a glass of milk?"

"Sure." When I bring it, she gets tears in her eyes. "You do so much for me, Kyle. You're like a little angel. I blow kisses to your picture every night before I go to sleep."

I want to cry. Neediness and gratitude. No wonder I'm a prisoner here.

There's a new class of beginners here, except poor old Hector. I recognize the kid who tried to get into our class who was underage. He must have turned eighteen. "David Steele!" I call out to him.

"Hi." He sticks out his hand to me. "I saw you in the June show. You were awesome, man."

Another fresh face speaks up. "Yeah, Jeff says you're the best he's ever coached."

I glance at, and then turn away from, Jeff's shit-eating grin. "What about Danny Battaglia?" I can't resist asking.

"He sucks!" says a third greenhorn. "Last show, he sneezed when Rat Boy put the rat on him."

I laugh uncontrollably. I didn't go to the two shows Danny was in. Too busy and bitter.

"Hey, Jeff," I say. "So you've paid these little marks to flatter the pants off me. Very nice of you, but let's get to work. Where's Hector?"

"He's changing," Jeff says with significant inflection. Hector used to wear street clothes to practice. He couldn't afford any gear. On cue, he comes out of the locker room in some nice gray sweat shorts and real wrestling boots. He's been working on his upper body and looks great. I'm impressed. He comes and gives me a big silent hug. "How's your grandma?" he asks me.

People usually don't ask me this, and that really pisses me off. "She's okay, Hector, thanks for asking. What's going on with you?"

He rolls his eyes. "You'll see."

I really admire this guy. How can he do it, keep showing up when he's always at the bottom of the class, never moving on? Now he's watching a whole new crop of kids go past him, and yet he shows up every day. Where does that come from?

Jeff, Hector, and I climb through the ropes. The kids sit on the front bleachers. Jeff puts a protective arm around Hector's shoulders and begins. "The problem seems to be that he can't do any kind of backward rotation. He can do a front flip like you wouldn't believe, but any back flip—shooting star, moonsault, you name it—and he freezes up and can't go though with it. True, Hec?"

"True." Hector sighs. "My brain says go. My feet say no."

This seems funny. Lots of people have a block on any kind of flip because they're scared to take their feet off the ground, but if Hector can do a front flip, why can't he do a back flip?

"Have you let him do it with a spotter? Or a table?" I ask Jeff. Sometimes you need to know something is under you while you learn the move.

"Yep," Jeff says. "He freezes. He won't go."

"I try, I really do," Hector says.

"I don't doubt that," I tell him. One thing Hector does is try. He's no coward. I can't crack the case. No wonder Jeff is frustrated. "Show me your front flip, Hector," I say, basically stalling for time.

"Okay." He executes a rotation and nails the landing perfectly.

"Okay!" I say. I go around behind him and put my arms in the small of his back. "Now, just reverse it, Hector. I've got you. You can't land wrong because I've got you. Just don't think. Go!"

He stands there. He bends his knees. He straightens his knees. "Can't."

I notice all the other beginners drinking this in. Every one of those little creeps can probably already do this.

"I know you can do this, Hector," I say. "There's really no difference between a front flip and a back flip except—" Then I get it. "Jeff. It's the blind spot. Maybe he can do the front flip because he can see the floor and know it's there. But rotating back, you have to look at the ceiling, and maybe he's real dependent on his eyes to guide him."

"That makes sense," Jeff says. "Okay, Hector. You gotta trust the ground. It's not going anywhere. Just tell yourself your feet will hit the mat."

We try again. Hector mutters to himself that he knows the mat is there. Nothing.

There has to be a way. "Okay," I say to Jeff. "If he's too dependent on his eyes, what about this? What if we blindfold him and have him do the front flip? His body already knows how to do that and we can teach his eyes that they aren't important."

Jeff shrugs. "Worth a try."

We tie a bandanna over Hector's eyes. I try not to notice how he looks like the victim of a firing squad now. I'm so grateful that this new class doesn't have any Dannys or Troys, who would be jeering and calling names at this point.

Hector gets ready to do his front flip. Nothing happens. "Aw shit. Now I can't do that either!" he yells.

Jeff laughs. "Well, you've proved your theory. But now he's screwed up for two moves instead of one."

"No!" Hector shouts. "Wait. I'm GOING to do it!" He is really angry, but that can be good. Adrenaline can push you right over an obstacle. You can almost see the energy building up in his body, and then he yells "now!" and jumps, rotates forward, and lands, a little two-footed, but he lands.

"Yes! Yes! Yes!" Jeff runs and hugs him and starts to take off the blindfold.

"Wait!" Hector shouts. "I'm going to do it backward. Now!" He jumps, rotates backward. He overrotates and lands on his knees, but it's good enough. He pulls off the blindfold, and we see tears. "I did it!" he roars. "I did it!"

Jeff and I both hug him. His classmates are cheering. "Thanks," Jeff says to me.

"Yes," Hector whispers. "Thank you."

I end up sitting in on the rest of the class, because Ophelia agreed to watch Chantal for the full time and because—yes, Jeff, you bastard—it was the most fun I'd had in three months. Jeff works with the younger guys on one side of the ring, and on the other, for the next hour, there's Hector doing his back flip over and over and over, like a windup toy gone mad. I stare at him, trying to understand what would make him knock himself out like this for nothing. He'll probably never make it to the pros. In fact, I'm not sure he could even make it to the intermediate class. He's too old, he has too little talent and not enough time. There's nothing to make him put up with all this physical stress and pain except that he likes to challenge himself. I remember what he wrote about himself on that card—*pit bull*. He was right.

Near the end of our time, one of the kids comes up to me. "Would it be, like, totally super annoying if I asked for your autograph?" he says and blushes like I'm a girl he's asking out.

I get up and sling my bag over my shoulder. "I'll give it to you," I say. I point up to the ring where Hector is still flipping. "But if you were really smart you'd ask for his."

* * *

Ophelia's reading a book when I get back.

"She's taking a nap," she says quietly. "She wanted to wash her hair so we played beauty parlor."

"Thank you." I bring her a bottle of water, and one for myself, and sit on the couch beside her. She smells like coconut and the edges of her hair brush my arm, but all my feelings are up in my head. None down where it would do some good.

"Did you enjoy the class?"

"Yes."

"Did you wish you were still taking classes?"

"Yes."

"Kyle, I know you're tired of hearing this but—"

I put up my hand. "I know."

"You know what?"

"I know this isn't how an eighteen-year-old is supposed to be living his life. I know I've gotten myself pinned down here by a lot of feelings I don't even understand. I know I need to do something about it, but I've been scared to take the first step. But now I'm going to do it."

She cradles my arm in hers. "What are you going to do?"

"I'm going to blindfold myself," I say. "And then I'm going to call my mother."

Chapter 13

I dial my mother's number in Connecticut. Her machine picks up. My fingers tighten on the receiver. She always has these totally irritating outgoing messages. First I hear a bunch of chimes, then a sound like wind blowing in the desert. Then her voice. "We can't answer you now. We are swept away in the throes of creation, we are lost in the void of bliss, we are searching for our truest selves. If you leave your name and number and if we return to this plane, we'll get back to you." *Beeeeep.*

I appreciate the beep. It's loud and rude, like an audience booing what it's just heard. I take a minute to push down my anger before I record.

"This is Kyle. You know, your son. I need to talk to you. Hope you make it back to this dimension okay." All right, I couldn't resist that.

* * *

Three hours later she calls back. I'm peeling potatoes for a pot roast. I need to start cooking more to get Chantal's appetite going. I make a promise to myself that I'll only eat carrots and a little of the meat myself. No potatoes.

I know from the caller ID it's her. "Hello?"

"Oh, Kyle. I was so touched by your call. How could you have known?"

"Known what?"

"You sensed I was in crisis. Genaro has left me."

I nick my hand with the peeler and put my work aside. This requires concentration. "What left you?"

"Genaro! Oh, Kyle, I thought he was a spiritual person, a soul mate! He took my jewelry box! I had to make a police report! There's a quartz pendant in there I use to balance my energy, and he knows that!"

"This is the reflexology guy?" I'm totally derailed.

"Yes! It was I who suggested he go into reflexology because I thought he was so sensitive. I feel like a fool!"

Trust your feelings, Mom. "Well, that's a shame. The reason I called—"

"It's so comforting to know that you sensed my distress and called me. Even though your grandmother raised you, I feel we'll always have a special bond, don't you?"

"Yes, I feel that bondage, too. Juliana, the reason I called . . ." I get a little weak-kneed and have to sit down. "We need to talk about Chantal. She's been sort of . . . declining—"

"What?"

I know I should have called her from the hospital when it happened. I just assumed she wouldn't care.

"She's kind of . . . deteriorating." I lower my voice, even though I know Chantal can't hear me. "Her memory, her balance, just her general . . . vitality. The doctors call it vascular dementia. She pretty much needs round-the-clock care."

"What are you talking about? My mother is the most vibrant woman alive."

Boy, am I sick of hearing that word. "She was, yes. She's eighty-six, Mom, I mean, Juliana. Things are changing. And now she's been having things called TIAs. They're like little strokes. But even before that—"

"Why are you telling me all this?"

I stand up. "What do you mean, why am I telling you all this? Because she's your mother!"

"Kyle, you don't know everything about the relationship between Chantal and me. She made some mistakes as a mother—"

"Well, so did you!" *Oops.* I swore I wasn't going to say stuff like that, but it just leaked out. And now that it is out, I just keep going. "But if you needed something I would hope I'd feel some kind of responsibility to you! And I would hope you feel that way about Chantal."

"Is this about money?" Her whole voice has gotten low, wary. A picture flashes in my mind of Whisker-Biscuit, poking around his cage, looking for the door.

"No, it's not about money. It's about me needing somebody to share this incredibly huge, freaking BURDEN with!" *Oh, God, I really yelled out that word. Please, God, don't let Chantal have heard that.* "I just graduated high school, and I can't go to work or school or anything because I have to take care of her twenty-four-seven. I'm a prisoner here. And I don't even know if I'm doing the right things. Like, should I make her get out of bed if she doesn't feel like it? Or, she feels safer taking sponge baths instead of showers because she's afraid of falling and obviously I can't go in there with her but—"

"I can't believe you're talking about Chantal."

"That's because you aren't here."

There's a long silence. I ride it out.

"Kyle, I know this question is going to make you mad, and I know I should know the answer: How old are you now?"

"Eighteen." It doesn't make me mad at all. It's what I expect.

She makes a noise, like she's flipping pages. Probably

her cosmic agenda book. "Do you want me to come to Florida?"

"Yes." I sink back into the chair.

"I don't have a show coming up until January. And I guess I could get someone to feed the lizards—"

I don't have the strength to ask what lizards. I just sit quietly while she thinks out loud.

"I hope this won't mess up my complaint to the police. Because I feel that I need justice to get psychological closure. Oh, God, what if Genaro breaks into the house while I'm gone . . ."

I play elevator music in my head. Chantal used to play these great old LPs for me when I was a kid. *The Girl from Ipanema.*

". . . and just let her stay in the house. She'll enjoy using my pool. She doesn't have one . . ."

But each day when she walks to the sea, she looks straight ahead, not at me . . .

". . . hoping to have the trees trimmed this month, but . . ."

She smiles! But she doesn't see . . . she just doesn't see . . .

". . . probably by the end of the week."

"Great. Give me your flight number when you get it."

"You can't pick me up at the airport?"

"We don't have a car. We live on a fixed income. But

actually, I have a friend who might pick you up. Let me ask her."

"Your girlfriend?"

"Yeah." For just that split second I feel like a real son talking to his real mother.

"What's she like?"

Very feminine for a pro wrestler. "You'll meet her. Call me back when you know your timetable."

"Okay, Kyle. Good-bye."

"Good-bye, Juliana." I wanted to say Mom, but not for the right reason, just to annoy her. After I hang up I feel sort of light-headed. The first thought that crosses my mind is this: *If she's staying here, I could get away and take a couple of wrestling classes.*

Ophelia and I lie on the couch together, our legs entwined, eating popcorn, basking in the soft flicker of the TV set. This is sacred time—Monday night—*RAW* is on.

"Do you want to talk about your mother coming?" Ophelia whispers. Chantal is a very sound sleeper, but we always whisper anyway. I wonder how people with children handle all the private stuff they have to talk about. Do they whisper all the time, or do they just give up and let the kids hear? Is there any way to have a family without somebody getting hurt?

"No." I stuff in popcorn like I'm starving. Popcorn is good because you can eat a lot of it without racking up too many calories.

"You have a lot of feelings bottled up." She goes on like she hasn't heard me. "Don't you want to sort them out?"

I sigh. She's deliberately chosen a hardcore match neither of us care about, so I can't shush her. "It isn't good to sort *everything* out," I tell her. "Like, supposing there was an explosion at the water treatment plant. You don't want to sort that out. You just want to clean it up real fast and pretend it never happened."

I thought that was kind of brilliant, but she's still playing deaf. "Naturally you're angry with your mother for abandoning you—"

"For creating me artificially and then abandoning me," I correct. "Have you ever read *Frankenstein*? You know, not the movie but the book. He makes the monster for his own ego and then the monster is all, like, "Daddy, Daddy," and the guy runs for the hills. That's my mom."

She laughs. "I guess it's hard not to have any sense of your father at all."

Pass the popcorn, please. "Yeff. Yeff, it is."

Women are vicious tacticians. Don't ever let them fool you. Ophelia lets a full five minutes go by with nothing but the sound of me stuffing my face and then her little voice floats out over the Twix commercial. "I guess that's why Chantal is so important to you."

I don't have to cry. If I chew a big enough wad of popcorn it will reverse the facial convulsing process necessary for crying. "Duh, duh, and duh," I respond.

"And that's why you're trying to sacrifice your whole life for Chantal. Because you'd rather do that than be an abandoner like your mother."

I focus on the Twix commercial. *Chewy, chewy, chocolate chewy.*

"I'm going to keep talking till you say something," Ophelia warns. "You didn't just call your mother to get her to step up to the plate for Chantal. You want her to help you, too."

I gently untangle my legs, stand up, and stretch.

"Don't shut down, Kyle. Talk to me."

But I can't. My vocal chords are paralyzed. I take a few deep breaths. "I would never"—I rasp like a snake—"accept help from that woman!"

"Then how come you called her?"

I pound my heart. "Because it's her fucking mother!" I scream. *Oh, God, I'm doing it again. Please, God, give me a pass on that one, too.* "Not mine!" I whisper loudly. "Doesn't she have some responsibility? Doesn't she care? Couldn't she show some tiny amount of interest?"

171

"Are you talking about her showing interest in Chantal or in you?"

I start walking around. "Do you know what you should do, Ophelia? You should set up a little stand on the sidewalk. Psychiatric Advice Five Cents. Like in the cartoon. What's your problem that you think you can sit there and judge me and my thoughts and feelings?"

She waits a minute. She's an expert in knowing when to not provoke a violent person. "I have a stake in this, Kyle. You don't know how to take care of other people without sacrificing yourself. You think abandonment or total sacrifice are your only choices. Because that's all you ever saw. If we're ever going to—"

I have to laugh, watching her face as she realizes she needs to backpedal.

"It's important for you to learn, Kyle, how to take care of other people without losing yourself."

"Chantal is totally helpless. I have to do practically everything for her. How am I supposed to go out and have a career if I can't leave her alone?"

"If she's that helpless, she needs assisted living. Or adult day care."

"I will never do that. I will never hand her over to someone else."

"Do you see? You're afraid of being like your mother."

I forget those promises to God and explode. I grab

Ophelia's shoulders and shake my point in. "I am NOTHING like my mother! Don't you ever, EVER say that again. You BITCH!"

Oh, shit. Now I'm not upset about what Chantal might have heard. Ophelia definitely heard me, and that means we're through. Women never forgive things like that. Now she'll definitely get what she wanted because here I go, crying like a baby, face-crumpling, knee-buckling, tear-blinded, throat-closing crying.

Subliminally I hear Jason Quest's music hit. Shit. That was the one segment I wanted to see.

Ophelia gets up somewhere behind me. I suppose she'll go home now and chalk me up as another abusive, addictive (popcorn this time, not beer) guy that she escaped from. If she had any girlfriends, they'd throw her a party and congratulate her.

But no, she's kneeling behind me, wrapping her arms around me.

"I'm sorry." I sob like a stupid baby.

"Okay."

"I'm a horrible person."

"You are, but you have good points, too."

I hear the crowd pop on TV.

"What's going on?" I sniffle.

"Quest did a suicide dive."

"Cool."

She lets go, stands up. "I'll get some Kleenex."

I drag my worthless ass to the couch again. Jason Quest is amazing tonight. His feet hardly touch the mat. Everything looks so effortless for him. You always feel that he loves being out there, drawing energy from the screaming crowd.

Ophelia plops a box of tissues in my lap.

"I'll never say that word again," I tell her.

"Forget that. We have way more important problems than that."

Very few things can make me turn my eyes from Jason Quest, but this does. "What are you talking about?"

She keeps watching the match. "You know what I'm talking about. We don't have a normal relationship anymore. You aren't even a normal person anymore. You're turning into some kind of a freaky hermit with no future. Don't you remember? You were supposed to be my good guy, the guy who proved I didn't make bad choices."

"So I'm a bad guy now?" This is just great. Can't one damn thing go right for me?

"No, I think you're a good guy. But you're really not that available anymore. I mean, I need you, too."

"So what are you saying?" I brace myself like she might hit me.

"I'm saying I hope your mother can provide some help, because if you keep on going like you're going, I have to do what I need to take care of myself. I'm just not going to cling on to another relationship that doesn't work."

"Well, if it's up to my mom to rescue the situation, let's give up right now," I say.

We watch Jason Quest fly around. I know one of us should say more, but I can't, and I think she won't. In the end, she's going to be like my career, another thing I didn't deserve to have in the first place. When the show's over, she just gets up and leaves without a word.

Chapter 14

I get kind of a shock when I see my mother at the airport. The last time I saw her, eight years ago, she had this long, brown ponytail and wire-sculpture earrings she made herself. She wore a black leotard and a big gypsy skirt. She was weird, but she was kind of cool.

Instead, this little old lady comes down the ramp. I mean, she couldn't be more than five foot two, and her hair is short and gray, and she's wearing that uniform that senior ladies in Florida wear—elastic-waist pants and a big, boxy shirt in scary, matching candy colors. Plus she has on, like, zero makeup and looks really old. I do a quick math problem and realize she's sixty-one! I grab Ophelia's hand for support, something I never do.

"Kyle, is that you?" Juliana calls, already holding out her carry-on for me to take. "I hardly recognize you!"

"Back at you!" I sling her bag over my shoulder, since Ophelia is trying to take it. She loves to show she's one of the boys, but I don't want her to be my mother's slave. That's my job. "Juliana, this is Ophelia. Ophelia, this is Juliana. God, this sounds like Shakespeare or something!"

Juliana is still staring at me. She's got a hand on each of my biceps. "You're so big! You were always such a slender little thing!"

The last time she saw me I was ten, I realize. No wonder she looks so much shorter! She didn't get little; I grew up. Still, she's got a lot of nerve making personal remarks right out of the gate!

I shake her off. "Well, it's hard to watch what you eat when you take care of someone."

"I think what Juliana means is that you have more muscles," Ophelia says. "You used to have a gymnast body, but now that you're wrestling—"

"Wrestling!" Juliana literally steps back. "You've been wrestling?"

It seems funny she doesn't know. But since I haven't told her, I guess I can't be mad. "Not amateur wrestling. I want to be a pro wrestler, like the guys on TV. I enrolled in a school. I was even in a show—"

"He was great!" Ophelia chimes in.

"But—" I continue as we walk to the baggage

claim. "As I said, I've had to quit all that because of Chantal."

"He *thinks* he has to quit all that," says Ophelia. I see she's going to get her agenda out bright and early. Like she thinks my mom will give a shit about my personal ambitions. That's a laugh.

"This is more than I can take in," says Juliana. Translation: That's enough about you—time to talk about me. "Did Kyle tell you what happened to me?"

"No, what?"

I focus on grabbing Juliana's bags. Easy to spot since, in the sea of black nylon, hers are blue and printed with dolphins. Where the heck do you go to get new age luggage? She's brought like four bags for this one-week stay. I guess she's planning on doing some scuba diving and folk dancing.

". . . and after I had paid for him to study reflexology!" Mom drones on.

"What's reflexology?" Ophelia asks. This should be good.

"Well, it's an ancient art and science. You see, the entire body is mirrored in the foot."

"What?"

"The sole of the foot. There's a connection between parts of the foot and different parts of the body."

"No there isn't!"

"Well, reflexology holds that there is."

"So you're saying there's some part of my foot that's connected to my heart."

I decide to sit on one of her larger bags and get comfortable. This is fun.

"Right."

"So is it like voodoo? I stomp my foot wrong, and I give myself a heart attack?"

"Well—"

"Or better yet"—Ophelia starts giggling—"instead of sex . . . what part of the foot is that? With the right kind of shoes . . . "

Juliana is getting pissed. "It isn't that kind of connection. It's an ancient art and science!"

"Yeah," my soon-to-be-ex-girlfriend guffaws. "Like prostitution."

I wait for the catfight to begin. But strangely, my mother laughs. "Well, that would explain why Genaro was so good at it!"

Before I know it, we're walking out the doors, Mom and Ophelia giggling and jostling each other like old friends. Me tagging behind, carrying all the bags.

Ben is babysitting Chantal today so we can all go to lunch and talk about her. Ophelia picked the restaurant downtown, the kind of restaurant women love, where there are about a hundred gay waiters hovering at all times, trying to fill your water glass or put pepper on something for you. Yuck.

Mom is explaining her "art" to Ophelia, so I have time to wage my internal struggle with the menu. I know I should have the salad with the salmon fillet on it, but they have pot roast. What difference does it make anyway? I'm never going to be a wrestler, and I'm looking at a totally aggravating week coming up. I need gravy!

"My last series was called *Frozen Moments*," Juliana explains. "I was trying to take images of motion"—her hands flutter all around—"and *stop* them at the very most telling point. In every sequence of motion, I believe, there is this optimal second that sums up the entire sequence. Parallel to the epiphany in literature. For example, a female pairs skater, going into the death spiral—the most significant moment is when she relinquishes control to her partner and her own momentum."

"And they all lived happily ever after," I say. "Mom, are you sure you shouldn't have been, like, a professor or a lawyer or something? Then you could talk all day and get paid for it."

"No, wait, this is interesting." Ophelia lays a hand on my arm. "I mean, think of wrestling. The frozen moment is the one when you see all the fans' cameras going off. Like in your frog splash, when you're in the air and at your full extension."

"Wow, you sound like a big fan of wrestling yourself, Ophelia," says Juliana.

Maybe I'll get the Cobb salad. It's still a salad, but it has bacon and blue cheese.

"No, Mrs. Bailey. I'm a wrestler, too. I met Kyle in wrestling school."

"You're kidding!"

Ophelia grins. She loves to shock people. "No, really."

Before we can explore that, the waiter, Bobby, comes over.

"We'll have a bottle of Sonora Cabernet," Ophelia says. "This is my treat, guys. And I'll have the pot roast."

You bitch.

"Oh, me too," says Juliana.

I grit my teeth. "I'll have the salmon fillet salad," I croak like a desiccated frog.

Bobby laughs. "Can't tell the boys from the girls here!" And off he goes.

"Good for you, Kyle!" Ophelia says quickly.

"Not so good for you. What's with the wine?"

"We're celebrating. This is a family reunion."

My mother and I exchange glances. For once we agree. That was a crock.

I don't want to lecture Ophelia about the wine in front of my mother, so I switch gears, hoping the alcohol won't mess us all up and turn this lunch into a Pier Six brawl.

"Okay," I say. "Let me just bring you up to speed on Chantal."

"All of this is just so hard for me," Juliana begins, taking a sip of the wine Ophelia is already sucking back. "I did some calculations on the plane, and I realized she's eighty-six years old. Did you realize she's that old, Kyle?"

"Yes, of course I did," I say, diving into the salmon fillet. "I live with her."

Juliana goes all dreamy-eyed. "She used to make these beautiful dresses for me when I was a little girl. Make them. Nobody does that anymore."

I try the wine. "Nowadays it's hard to find people who will even raise their own kids."

Ophelia kicks me. I raise my glass to her.

It doesn't matter, anyway. Sarcasm is wasted on narcissists because they aren't really listening.

"She would bake these delicate little almond cookies. I remember coming home from school on rainy days . . ."

There's nothing but vegetables and salmon in this salad. Not even a freaking crouton. "Remember when I would come home from school on rainy days?" I said. "Oh, wait. You weren't there."

That, she heard. In our lunch, I guess, this would be a frozen moment.

"I thought we were supposed to be talking about

Chantal." Juliana's eyes get steely and cold. I remember this look, and it scares some old, old part of me.

Ophelia pours everyone another glass. "Neither one of you is talking about what Chantal needs now."

"She needs me now," I say, meeting steely eyes with steely eyes. "And that's why I'm taking care of her. I guess I must take after Daddy's side that way."

"Okay, Kyle." Juliana puts down her fork. "If you need to get this out of the way first, just come out and do it. I admit it. I was a complete failure as a mother. I did, indeed, fail you. It was nothing personal, but I realized I wasn't cut out to be a mother—"

"That right there!" The flat of my hand hits the table. "Stop right there! This is what I don't understand about you. How can you just decide you aren't cut out for something that's your responsibility? How do you think you can just walk away from stuff you're supposed to do because it doesn't suit your little temperament? Don't you think that's, you know, wrong?"

"In your case? No, I don't think that was wrong. Chantal was a much better caretaker than I ever could have been. She's so well suited to all the little domestic things. Not all women have magical, automatic caretaking skills. That's a myth that society foists on us. Am I right?" She turns to Ophelia, who was swigging away and who now freezes like a deer in headlights.

"Maybe Kyle just wants you to say you're sorry."

"Yeah, that'll fix it." I stuff a huge forkful of salmon and greens into my mouth.

"Kyle"—Juliana tries to touch my hand, but I put it in my lap—"I am sorry. I know we both wish I could have been a better mother. But knowing myself, I know I did the right thing for you. You deserved to be well cared for, and I realized that I wouldn't—couldn't—do that, and I knew someone who could because she had done it for me. I know why you're angry with me, but wasn't that the right choice? If you'd been with me, you'd be angry for all different reasons. I would have missed all your gymnastics meets while I was out chasing younger men. If you'd stayed with me, you would've hated me."

There's a very long silence while I refrain from stating the obvious.

"Let's bring it back to Chantal," says Dr. Phil/Ophelia. She sets down her wine. I pick up my fork. "Kyle is taking great care of her for now, but I know for a fact the job is getting harder and harder all the time. And, Juliana, you certainly will understand this—it isn't right that he forget his career and his dreams and become a full-time caretaker. That's the wrong thing for an eighteen-year-old boy to do."

My mother tears off a corner of bread and butters it. "Maybe he's just doing this to make a big display of what *good* people are supposed to do. Maybe the whole thing is just being staged for my benefit."

"And maybe this is not about you at all!" The words start exploding out of me faster than I can think. "Maybe, Juliana, there are things going on in the world that have absolutely nothing to do with your 'art' or your 'choices' or your 'boyfriends' or anything. Maybe while you were finding yourself, Chantal and I built up a relationship that neither of you understands. Maybe because she *was* there for me all the way, I want to be there all the way for her. Maybe that's what I think I owe her. And maybe in this situation, you're just irrelevant, Mom!"

It's around this time that I see everyone in the restaurant is staring at us. Me, actually. You know how it is. Some speeches that you make absolutely call for you to exit. I couldn't have said that stuff and then sat there munching my salad. So I get up and march out into the Florida sun, and then I realize I don't have a car. I kind of want to laugh as I review my options. Go back and finish lunch. Call a cab and spend most of the grocery money. Or take my old friend—the city bus—for a two-hour ride back home to Coral Springs. I fish in my pockets for chump change.

When Ophelia finally brings Juliana home—they went to a movie!—Chantal doesn't have a clue who she is.

"You'll have to take it up with my grandson. I don't

understand what you want," she says with a dismissive wave of her hand. I love it.

We all—Juliana, Chantal, Ophelia, Ben, and I— have dinner together. I make spaghetti. Ophelia suggests breaking out another bottle of wine, but I tell her absolutely not. Then, like the hypocrite I am, I have two platefuls of food.

"When are you going to tell Kyle?" Ophelia says to Ben. I'm starting to see her as a real instigator.

Ben, now that I think of it, did act like he had something to say all afternoon. "Is something wrong?" I ask him.

"I'm quitting wrestling." He lowers his eyes.

"What? Why? You're good!"

He dips some bread in sauce and drags it around his plate. "I'm not cut out for it, man. I don't have the heart for the business. Every bone in my body hurts, and it keeps getting harder all the time. I don't want to be on the road all my life—"

"How can you do this?" For the second time today I feel myself going out of control without really knowing why. "Do you know how many people would kill to have your chance?"

"What are you talking about?" Ophelia says. "You dropped out, too."

It seems crazy to jump up and walk out on my

second meal of the day. "You really want to be a librarian all your life?" I ask him.

"Yep," he says. "I love the books, and I love the kids. You gotta do what you love."

I sort of deflate and stare at my plate. "I'm doing what I love," I say. For emphasis, I look up at Chantal, who is fishing an ice cube out of her drink with her fingers. "How you doing, sweetheart?"

She looks at me blankly. "What?"

After everyone leaves and Chantal has her bedtime ice cream, the only daily routine she never forgets, it's just me and Mommie Dearest, watching TV in the dark. It's downright spooky. I mean, if I wanted to, I could pretend she had never dumped me off and here we were having family time. In that universe, she'd be a little sad tonight, thinking about me going off to college soon.

"There was just a little ice cream left in that container," I say. "Do you want it?"

"No, go ahead."

Actually, there's quite a bit left in the container, but there won't be when I'm finished. For good measure, I pour some Hershey's in there, too. When I'm back, happily stuffing myself, Juliana slides her eyes sideways at me. "There's something I want to ask you."

Kiss your ass? Peel you a grape? Scatter rose petals at your feet? "What?"

"Ophelia said you have a tape of that wrestling show you were in. I'd like to see it. I'd like to see what you do."

Of all the things she could have said, this one was not on my radar screen. "Why?"

"Because she says you're really good. And I don't see how anyone could possibly be talented at something as silly as wrestling. So I want to see."

She's calling me out! She wants to throw down! This is something I can respond to. "Watch and learn," I say. I go to the shelf where I have all the tapes of my gymnastics meets and, at the end of the row, my GCW tape. That's all you have if you're an athlete. Trophies and tapes.

"I'll just start at the beginning," I tell her. "I'm the first match. It's called the curtain puller. They put something interesting on to get the crowd hot from the start."

"I see," says Miss PBS, pulling her half glasses down on her nose into the judgmental position. I start the tape, feeling oddly hot and shaky.

The camera work is shaky, too. "Who's filming this?" she asks.

"Quentin Tarantino. He likes to film wrestling shows on his days off. This is a shoestring operation, Juliana. You won't see any match dissolves or extreme close-ups."

"I was just asking!" She's watching little Chelsea sing the national anthem.

"Some of these shows are broadcast on the Sunshine Network," I say. "But not this one."

Rat Boy comes out to boos and hisses. "That's my opponent and my boss," I explain.

"Rat Boy?"

"Yeah. See? He has a rat." What does our quirky profession look like to an outsider? Even worse, a pseudo-intellectual outsider like my mother.

"Okay, here I come."

"Barnaby the Scribbler?"

"The announcer got it wrong."

"Oh, my God!" She's seeing me now, finally. "Look at you! Look at those muscles!"

Oh, yeah, she's an expert in young male bodies. I forgot that. "I was working out a lot back then."

"What are they chanting?"

" 'Who are you?' It's a way they have of honoring a newcomer."

"Oh! Look at that! That was cool!" She's referring to my ring entrance.

"That's nothing," I say. "Keep watching." What's wrong with my face? Dear God, I think I'm smiling at her. But I can't help it. Seeing this tape always makes me so goddamn happy.

"Oh! Oh! My God, is he hurting you? He isn't really kicking you, is he?"

"We aren't permitted to reveal our secrets."

I watch the TV light flicker on her stunned face. She squeals at my drop kick, shrieks at my flying head scissors, gasps, along with the crowd, at my frog splash.

"This is a bit like the Kabuki!" she exclaims.

I don't know what the Kabuki is, but from the look on her face, it's something good.

I'm getting "ratified" now. "Oh, how can you stand that!" she cries.

"It makes the fans happy."

"You're really acting! It's like acting and dance and acrobatics. I had no idea."

The match is over. I stop the tape.

"You're a performer, Kyle," she says. "You're a born performer."

"Well, thanks. That's what my teachers said, too, but of course now—"

"No, no! You have to do this! We're going to find a way to help you do this. You can't waste a talent like that. That audience loved you!"

It hits me all at once. Such a clear, perfect thought I want to blurt it out, but I don't think she'd understand. I suddenly realize that even if she'll never be the mother I want her to be, she might have made a really terrific father.

Chapter 15

We eat dinner in silence. As the week wore on, everyone seemed to slow down, including Chantal, who won't even come to the table tonight. She says she already had dinner. I tried to argue with her, but she was positive. Sometimes I try to look at the world through her eyes. I picture it like a dark tunnel where you see a light at the end and maybe people doing something but you can't tell what. When I talk to Chantal these days, I get in the tunnel myself, and it makes me so heavy and sad I sometimes just have to walk away. Just to feel alive again.

Juliana leaves day after tomorrow. That makes me sad, too, strangely enough. So I'm shoveling mashed potatoes into my mouth, and Ophelia, who's having dinner with us, is on her fourth glass of wine.

"You're totally messing up your training," I tell her when I can't stand to watch anymore.

She was kind of slumped over, but she sits up real straight. "I only take advice on training from people *in* training," she shoots back.

More silence. Disturbing that Juliana looks like the most functional person in the house at the moment. "I've been here a week, Kyle," she says abruptly. "And we haven't come to any conclusions about Chantal."

I don't stop eating to talk. "What's to conclude? The doctors say she'll probably keep getting worse and worse. What am I supposed to do?"

"Well, for one thing, you need help in taking care of her. How long has it been since she's had a bath?"

I stare at my plate, feeling ashamed, like I don't take baths. "She said she can wash up well enough at the sink. You don't expect me to give her a bath, do you? I'm doing the best I can!" The potatoes are all gone. I scrape desperately at my plate with my fork.

"You're an eighteen-year-old boy," Juliana says as my girlfriend nods drunkenly. "Your best isn't good enough here. She needs trained help at this point. I can afford—"

"Please don't do me any favors," I say. "I'll look into it myself."

"Why do you have to do everything?" says Ophelia. Usually she doesn't get noticeably impaired, but right now she's slurring. I wonder if she was drinking before she came over. "Don't you remember what we talked about? You're supposed to get some help so you can get back to your life."

"Chantal is my life," I say. "For as long as she needs me. She was there for me, I'm going to be there for her. Excuse me, I need to see if I can get her to eat something." I'm still hungry, so she must be starving.

My feet feel heavy and slow walking down the hall to her room. She's just lying on the bed, not even watching TV anymore. Lately, she can't remember which button to hit on the remote. She's just breathing and looking at the ceiling. "Chantal?"

She turns her head and looks at me. Maybe she's dehydrated.

"You want something to eat?" I ask. My tone is like begging. "Maybe a glass of water? Some ice cream?"

"What time is it?" her voice is weak and frail.

"Seven o'clock."

She turns her head the other way. "I'll just wait for breakfast."

I wonder if she thinks it's seven A.M. I get so tired trying to untangle what she says. Suddenly, standing there in the twilight room, I have no energy to speak. Or do anything. I give up and shuffle back to the dinner table.

They were whispering frantically about me, and they

stop the minute they hear me coming. Yes, I'm doing everything wrong. Why don't you guys try it?

Ophelia fills up another glass for herself. She's left quite a bit of food on her plate. I wonder if she's going to eat it. "Kyle, I think it's time for me to cash in on my ultimatum to you. Your mother is willing to pay for help for you, and you're refusing to take it. You promised me you were going to do something to improve this situation, and I told you I wasn't going to wait around and be ignored forever. This is for your own good, Kyle. Either you tell me right now you're going to hire an aide, or I'm out of here."

I imagine Chantal, frightened and confused, some strange woman forcing her into a bathtub. I waggle my fingers at Ophelia. "Have a great life."

She closes her eyes like I hit her. Then she gets up. "It was nice meeting you, Juliana," she says. I listen to the door slam, listen to her burn rubber. Too late, I wonder if she should have driven home by herself. I can't worry about everyone. . . .

"She was too good for me anyway," I say to Juliana. "That had to happen."

She takes one of those really deep breaths adults take when they're about to lecture your head off. It doesn't matter. She can say anything she wants. Nobody understands the box I'm in. I don't like it, I don't want it, but I don't have a damn choice.

"I want to tell you something about myself," she says.

No surprise there. But it's preferable to what's wrong with me.

"Did you ever wonder what my life was like before you were born?"

"Why should I?" That just came out. Like I said, I'm tired.

"I had you when I was forty-three. You never wondered why I didn't get married, what I was doing with my life?"

I just look at her.

"I was here, living in this house, doing what you're doing right now. Living for Chantal. Paying her back because she was such a great caretaker to me, too. When my father died, oh, Kyle, I wish you could have known him, he was a terrific man. In fact, now that you're older, you remind me of him. Anyway, when he died, she was devastated. He was her whole life. They adored each other. She had never made friends of her own. And when he died, she turned to me. She said, 'It doesn't matter. I'm not alone as long as I have you.'"

In spite of myself, I'm interested. "How old were you?"

"Eight."

"I'm sorry you had to lose your father that young." It's the decent thing to say.

"She planned all these trips for us to take together.

We went out to lunch at grown-up restaurants. Kyle, she made me take my father's place as her best friend. It made me into a weird kid. Other kids wouldn't be friends with me. She took me to the opera and stuff. What did I have in common with children? Mom and I grew together like one of those double pine trees."

"Okay, your childhood was sad, but—"

"No, it didn't end there. She didn't like my boyfriends. She said she'd be too lonely if I went away to college, so I went to community college. I wanted to be an artist, but she didn't like my supplies cluttering up the house. And every time I thought about asserting myself, I would think how she had lost her husband and I was all she had. Kyle, I was in a trap, just like you're in."

"She's not doing that to me!"

"Right. I agree. You're doing it to yourself, just like I did. When I got desperate, at forty-three, I thought if I had a child of my own, I'd have an excuse to have a home of my own. If I was taking care of you, she couldn't complain about me not taking care of her."

I notice it's gotten dark and we haven't turned on any lights. I stand up and flick on the bright, overhead kitchen lights. She winces.

"Great reason to have a kid."

"It's worse than that, Kyle. When I realized I was terrible at taking care of a child, she kept offering and offering, 'Come and move home. I'll help you.' So, well, Kyle, you know what I did. I gave you to her. Because that shut her up. She finally let me go because she got someone new to smother. And I ran like the wind. I've been making up for all those dutiful years, playing at being an artist, messing around with any man I think is cute, and you were here paying the price. And best of all, I could tell myself it was a win-win situation, that you were getting good care, she was happy, I was finally happy. I didn't think about you growing up. Or her growing old—"

I get up. Just because the pressure of everything she's saying seems to be about to explode inside of me. "I think if I just bring her a dish of ice cream, maybe she'll eat it," I say in a strangled voice. "I won't give her a choice."

I pick her favorite, butter pecan. I take a napkin and a spoon and head down the dark hall to the dark room. I turn on the lights.

"Oh, mercy!" She frets. "What now?"

"Ice cream," I say. "It's butter pecan because I know—"

"Juliana!" she bellows. I'm stunned. Most of the week she hasn't known who my mom is. Sometimes she goes back in time, so that must be it.

Juliana comes in. "What is it, Chantal?"

She hooks her thumb at me. "Some kid keeps coming in here bothering me. Can't you get rid of him?"

My knees go. Just like that, they give way and the ice cream goes all over the floor. I start to cry.

"Good Lord," Chantal exclaims. "There's something wrong with him!"

I get up and stagger out, blinded by tears. I make it halfway down the hall before my knees go again. She doesn't know me. The only person in this world who ever cared about me doesn't know me. I'm lost.

I hear Juliana quietly close Chantal's door and walk up behind me. I want to stop crying, but I can't. I feel like I'm dead, like I made a fatal mistake and now I'm dead. I feel Juliana put her arms around me. "I know, baby," she says. "I know."

Chapter 16

The next day I wake up with a terrible headache. I notice that Juliana's bags are not packed. Chantal is not in her room. I go out to the kitchen and find them both eating bagels. "Guess what?" Juliana says. "Chantal is moving to Connecticut to live with me."

"Yes," Chantal says. "This is my daughter."

"What's that going to solve?" I say weakly.

"Well, I can hire a full-time aide to take care of her, which you can't afford and are reluctant to do. And if and when she needs assisted living, I'll be strong enough to make it happen, which you won't."

I feel weird that she's saying this stuff out in the open right in front of Chantal. But then Chantal says, "I think it would be better if I went to this new school, because I don't know where my mother and father are right now."

"I owe you this, Kyle," says Juliana. "You know I do. And I can handle it. I've had years of practice in setting boundaries and making sure I get to live my own life. I want you to get some practice at it. And to be perfectly honest with you, I think this will be good for me, too. I'm really running out of enthusiasm for chasing after younger men. I sort of need a new direction."

All I can think of is this one time Chantal took me to the Kennedy Space Center to see the shuttle go up. She loved the space program, got mad whenever the funding was cut. She thought the astronauts were the modern equivalent of Columbus and Magellan. I remember watching the shuttle go up like a shooting star in reverse and Chantal holding me and saying, "You see? You can do anything in this world. Anything."

My mother interrupts my thoughts. "If you don't learn how to be happy now, Kyle, it will mess you up, forever. You need to trust me on this one."

"I think my mother and father will be along any time now to get me," Chantal says. "I saw them just the other day."

"Okay," I say. I look at Chantal. "I'll miss you. You know?"

"I'm not ready to get married, Dennis," she says.

I don't care if she understands or not. "You did a lot for me. I'll never forget it."

She laughs. "Oh, that was nothing."

Juliana turns to her. "You want to go back to your room and help me pack up your clothes?"

"You're taking her now?"

"I already arranged the plane tickets. Kyle, this is like pulling off a Band-Aid. The quicker we do it, the quicker we can all adjust."

I have tears in my eyes. "I don't know what to say."

She laughs just like her mother. "It's nothing. Anything else I can do for you?"

"Yes."

"What is it?"

"From now on, let me call you Mom."

Now it's her turn to cry.

"What a gloomy bunch!" says Chantal.

Gold Coast Wrestling is headquartered in a tiny office at the back of the Coral Springs Gymnasium. Hours are by appointment only, so both Jeff and Rat Boy know I'm coming.

Out front, in the gym, Jeff is subbing for the advanced class. Danny's in the ring. He looks so much more buff than the last time I saw him, it's like there's a glare of success coming off him. I put my head down, but that's no deterrent to a prick like him.

"Well, well, well, look what came crawling back! Too

bad your job is already taken!" He leans over the ropes as I walk by. I remember schoolyard bullies from years back and shiver a little.

Jeff runs to protect me. "How are you doing?" He thumps and pats me. "Listen, Rat Boy is going to give you a hard time, but I know he wants you back. You'll just have to power through this."

"I understand," I tell him. "He feels like I abandoned him. Nobody likes that."

I walk quietly to the back, accompanied by catcalls and insults from the other advanced students about what I'm probably going to do to try and get a job and how well suited I look for doing it. Lots of these guys have hated me all the way back to my first show. Some of them have been waiting years to get a spot in a show.

Usually the door is left open if someone's in there. Today it's closed. He isn't going to make this one bit easy for me. I knock.

"Who is it?" God, I've missed that horrible Brooklyn screech.

"It's me."

"Oh. Come in."

He's a businessman today, shirtsleeves and a tie that look weird with his black spiked hair. Reading glasses balanced on his narrow nose. "Well"—he tips back his chair—"if it isn't Barnaby the Scribbler."

"No," I say. "It's just some kid. Who wants a job."

He tips his head back, looks at me through the glasses. The gesture weirdly reminds me of Juliana. "I know lots of kids who want a job. What makes you so special?"

"I want it more than they do."

His chair drops back into place with a bang. "No, Kyle. No, I don't think you do. That's what I thought about you. Past tense. That's what Jeff told me about you, and it seemed like it was true. But I hand you a great spot in a show, hand it to you on a silver platter, and what did you do, Kyle? You spat on it. You spat on me!"

"No," I say, trying to look brave. "That's not what happened. My grandmother got . . . sick, and I didn't know what to do. I got . . . lost trying to do the right thing."

"So? What am I supposed to do if Granny gets sick again? Give you the Nobel Prize and try to book a show around you?"

"She's moving to Connecticut to live with my mother," I say. "It's . . . the best thing for her. I'm gonna be all yours now, if you'll have me. Because I've got nothing else."

"Yeah, right. The next thing, you'll marry Paula Pureheart and have a bunch of babies, and you'll want family leave. This is the circus, Kyle. If you want to join the circus, you have to cut your ties with the real world. I'm being serious with you now. All of us—Jeff, me, certainly the guys that work for Vince McMahon—I'm not saying they're all hard, but they have to have a certain kind of ruthlessness. Or this destroys them. I know you better now, and I don't know if you're the right kind of guy. That big heart won't go away just cause Granny goes to Connecticut. I love your talent, Kyle. I could make a lot of money with you, when you've had more experience. You could be the guy Jeff dreams of. The guy he trains who makes it to television. I'm not bullshitting you here. But we both have to see, all over again, that you really want this enough."

"I know that," I say. "I don't care if it takes time. If you give me the chance, you'll see. If you don't give me a chance, I'll find somebody else who will."

A little smile leaks around the corners of his mouth. Suddenly he jumps up as if to stop himself from giving in to me. He comes around the desk and gets right in my face. "Holy shit, Kyle. Look at you! You're fat!" He grabs the front of my shirt and holds it up. "How much weight have you put on?"

I back up and pull my shirt down, feeling my face get hot. "Twelve and a half pounds. But I—"

"Twelve and a half pounds! What were you doing with Granny? Eating bonbons and watching soap operas?"

"Look!" I yell at him. "I know how to cut weight!"

"Safely? Or are you going to be like Troy and hit the supplements? We kicked him out, you know. Caught him back on those things. So if you do it the healthy way, you know the math as well as I do. Two months—two shows—will go by before I can even consider using you! So now we're into next year. And I'm supposed to get all excited just because you want to come back? Let me tell you, buddy. You are starting from square one with me. Below square one. You get yourself back in a class and get rid of the rust and lose this disgusting fat and then, maybe then, I will be willing to look at you again as if I never knew you and then, maybe, maybe you will possibly have a chance to be in a show. Because you will have to convince me—not Jeff—me, all over again that I should invest my resources on a guy with a big soft heart and a weight problem—"

"I don't have—"

"My suggestion to you, Kyle, is that you get your ass out of here now and get into that class that's going on right now, because you haven't got a second to lose in trying to start looking like a wrestler again. And when you get home, here's a tip. Throw away all the chips."

I smile, because from Rat Boy, this is as close as you get to a hug and a valentine. "I hear you."

"God!" He sits back down and shakes out about twelve

Advil. "You kids will all be the death of me. I should have stayed in New York and gone into my father's mattress business. Then I'd be driving a good car and not a Saturn with a bunch of microphones in the back seat. Okay, why are you still here? Go!"

I turn to the door, laughing.

"Kid?"

I turn back.

"Okay, I'm going to give you one last thing. As an incentive. Your rival? Danny-boy? I hate him. He's a talented worker, but I hate him. If you do what you're supposed to do, it would be my total pleasure to give his spot to you. And that's still a big if."

"That would be my total pleasure, too," I tell him.

"And my rat can't stand him either," he mutters as I close the door.

I walk back out to a fresh chorus of jeers.

"Here comes Mrs. Rat Boy!"

"Look, he can hardly walk!"

"Maybe he had to do it with the rat!"

I ignore them and go straight to Jeff. "I know I'm out of shape, but can I be in this class? I'll work really hard to keep up."

"You bet." He slaps my shoulder. "Go change. We'll put you in the ring and see where you're at."

"Whooo, teacher's pet!"

"Change into a skirt!"

"No girls allowed!"

It's good to be home.

I'm a mess in the class, but I know what I need to do and I know how to do it. Coming out of the dressing room, I see Ophelia leaning against the wall.

"Need a ride home, sailor?"

"How'd you know I was here?"

She laughs. "Jeff, the happy-ending king, gave me a call. Said you were back. I'm not so sure. I watched the last five minutes of your class. Pretty pathetic."

"I know. I'm pathetic as a boyfriend, too. But I'm very motivated and eager to learn. I was on my way to your place to beg for forgiveness, but I stopped here first to get some knee pads."

She laughs. One thing in my favor is that I always crack her up. "You don't have to beg," she says. "You've been through a lot. So what's going to happen to Chantal?"

"It's a long story."

She takes my arm. "I've got a while."

Chapter 17

Valentine's Day falls on a Saturday this year, and believe it or not, there are a lot of people who will celebrate it by going to a wrestling show. Including me. Well, I have to go. I'm in it.

In the morning we all show up at the Coral Springs City Gymnasium to set up. Everyone helps: the promoters, the twenty-four wrestlers, and some of the students from Jeff's school who want to suck up.

I tape flyers all around the walls. Rat Boy, who is screaming at someone in another corner of the gym, is a big believer in flyers. We mail them out to loyal customers, stick them on windshields, tack them up at any store that will let us, and finally, when there are still hundreds left over we decorate the walls with them.

Gold Coast Wrestling

Presents:

LOVE HURTS!

Saturday, February 14th, 8 P.M., Coral Springs City Gymnasium
Featuring:

THE DEATH MACHINE VS. THE A-BOMB—
GCW Heavyweight Title

GLUTEOUS MAXIMUS VS. THE AMERICAN WAY—
Kiss My Ass Match

WAR OF THE ROSES—
Twelve-Woman Lingerie Match, NO HOLDS BARRED!

JOHNNY DOUBLETREE VS. SOME KID—
Balcony Match

Some Kid is my professional name. I feel like it's a sort of permanent tribute to Chantal and to staying humble. This is my second show. The first one was in January. I wrestled Danny and he tried so hard to mess me up they put him on a little time-out. I just hope he's not in the crowd tonight because he'll try to flip them to boo me. But it goes with the territory, I guess. He'll always think I screwed him over, when he did it to himself. And I'm sure if I stay in this business he won't be the only enemy I make.

"Kid!"

You make great friends, too. I turn around and see

my opponent for tonight, Johnny Doubletree. He's an incredible athlete, a full-blooded Seminole who got his start wrestling alligators for the tourists. He does very high-risk spots and is definitely considered one of GCW's rising stars. It's an honor they're pairing me with him, even though my job is, of course, to lose and continue his rise to stardom.

"Hey." I shake his hand. "Get a valentine this morning?" He just got married and talks about his sex life all the time.

"Three! How 'bout you?"

"Just one. But Ophelia and I have to do a show tonight." She moved in with me on New Year's Day, right after we both landed jobs at the same health club. You have to have a regular job to do this. I'm getting a whopping one hundred dollars for risking my neck on a bunch of ladders tonight.

"You okay she's in that match tonight?" he asks.

"No, I'm not okay, but you think I'm going to tell Ophelia I don't want her to be in her very first show? I'll just plug my ears when all the marks are catcalling her."

"What's she wearing?" he asks.

I sigh. "It begins already. Red garter belt and fishnets."

"Whoo!"

"Yeah, okay. Maybe I'll try to get your wife interested in wrestling."

"Don't you dare. It's really too bad the women have to do that stuff."

"I know. Most of them hate it, but Ophelia's an exhibitionist. She had the time of her life at Victoria's Secret, picking things out."

"You poor slob."

"It's okay. We're good for each other." We really are. She won't let me eat, and I won't let her drink. Our agreement is that we should both channel all of that energy into fantastic sex.

"All right," Johnny says. "I'm gonna go down and make sure they're putting the ladders in the right place for us tonight. Then let's walk through it one more time, just to be sure."

"I'll be here with my little roll of tape."

He slaps my shoulder. "I want to tell you something, kid. It's really been fun working out a program with you this month. You're one of the best workers I've ever seen. You know how to take care of yourself in the ring, and take care of the other person at the same time. That's rare."

"My grandmother taught me how to take care of other people," I tell him. And then I smile as I realize the other half of it. "And my mother taught me how to take care of myself."

"They did a great job," he says as he walks away.

"Hey!" he screams at the guy setting up the ring. "Don't shove the ladder in that far! You want me to ruin my back trying to drag it out? Let me show you!"

"Kid!" someone calls. "Telephone!"

I figure it's Ophelia. She went out shopping for shoes this morning because she has nothing suitable for her ho outfit. "Hey, baby," I growl into the receiver.

"Don't speak to your mother like that!"

"Mom!"

"I just called to wish you Happy Valentine's Day and tell you to break a leg tonight."

"No, no! That's actors, Mom. You don't tell a wrestler to have an injury!"

"Well, whatever."

"How's Chantal?"

"Okay. She does less and less, and the aides do more and more. But she was very happy with those chocolates you sent."

"Did she know who they were from?"

"Honey, don't torture yourself. You know—"

"I know. What else is going on?"

"I'm studying that tape you gave me. I want to do a sculpture of you doing that frog hop thing."

"Frog splash!"

"Whatever! How's Ophelia?"

"Oh, great. She's wrestling tonight in a garter belt."

"Well, whatever makes you kids happy. I'll let you go. I know you're busy."

"Okay, Mom. And . . . thanks."

"For calling?"

"No. Just thanks."

The "curtains" tonight are streamers of red tinsel. I stand on the other side, trying to stay loose, getting in character. Trying not to get distracted by Ophelia in her garter belt giving me a hug.

"Soooooome Kid!"

I'm thrilled to hear the pop when I go through the streamers and into the blaze of the spotlight. For a second, I can't see anything, but I pose and smile to the sea of blackness and flashbulbs that resolves into a bunch of kids with their hands stretched out to me. I try to touch as many of them as I can.

I hear the unmistakable voice of Danny somewhere behind me, trying to start up "Who are you?" chants, but they drown him out with "Some Kid! Some Kid!" I climb into the ring and look back toward the bleachers. I see my old friend Ricky and all the guys from the gymnastics team. I see Ben, who has quit the business to go back to the library. I see David Steele, who has made me his role model for success. I see Hector, who is still slogging away in the beginner's class. I see Ophelia,

Jeff, and Rat Boy near the entrance ramp, leading the cheers.

I get up on one of the ring posts and pose for the fans. I'm rewarded by a frenzy of flashbulbs. A stranger has made a sign for me. They're all chanting my name, "Some Kid! Some Kid! Some Kid!" They know who I am. This is where I belong.

Acknowledgments

Thanks to the WWE, WCW, ECW, and all the Indies for years and years of inspiration and entertainment. Thanks to the Miami Jewish Home and Hospital for the Aged for helping me through the toughest year of my mother's life and for giving me the resources and tools to understand. Special thanks to Dr. Marc Agronin, Lisa Lewis, Hazel Dunn, Rachel Bishop, Victoria Wiley, Mildred Byrd, Fred Stock, Joyce Kutchner, Dr. Ricardo Blondet, Dr. Morton Getz, Dr. Michael Silverman, Audrey Coney, Emanie Sylvain, Andre Morrison, Joe Goelz, and Irving and Hazel Cypen: I will never forget your kindnesses to me. Thanks to Laurie Friedman for that day we had lunch and I told you the idea for the book and you told me I had to write it. Thanks to Heidi Boehringer and Alex Flinn for excellent critiques and suggestions. Thanks to George Nicholson for finding exactly the right editor for this book, and thanks to Kate Farrell for being that editor. Thanks to AA Michael for very special favors. Most of all, thanks to my tag-team partner, Jay, who is always there, watching my back and cheering me on.